PRAISE FOR JEFFRY W. JOHNSTON'S

THE TRUTH

"What a fast-paced read! All Chris needs to do is tell the truth. But the truth isn't always a simple thing. What really happened the night a boy died at Chris's house? The end will leave you gasping."

—April Henry, *New York Times* bestselling author of
A Deadly Business and *The Body in the Woods*

"A tough, fast, twisty little brawler of a book."

—*Booklist*

"This captivating thriller keeps the pacing fast, the tension high, and the emotions raw."

—*Bulletin of the Center for Children's Books*

"Recommended for readers who enjoy edgy thrillers."

—*School Library Journal*

"An excellent novel that will keep the reader going and guessing up until the very end."

—*VOYA*

ALSO BY JEFFRY W. JOHNSTON

The Truth

FOLLOWING

FOLLOWING

JEFFRY W. JOHNSTON

sourcebooks
fire

Published by Sourcebooks Fire, an imprint of Sourcebooks, Inc.
P.O. Box 4410, Naperville, Illinois 60567-4410
(630) 961-3900
Fax: (630) 961-2168
sourcebooks.com

Library of Congress Cataloging-in-Publication data

Names: Johnston, Jeffry W., author.
Title: Following / Jeffry W. Johnston.
Description: Naperville, Illinois : Sourcebooks Fire, [2019] | Summary:
    Amateur investigator Alden Ross thinks he witnessed a murder, but when the
    victim shows up alive, he must figure out what he could have seen and what
    the school's most popular couple is hiding.
Identifiers: LCCN 2018033686 | (pbk. : alk. paper)
Subjects: | CYAC: Detectives--Fiction. | Murder--Fiction. | Mystery and
    detective stories.
Classification: LCC PZ7.1.J645 Fo 2019 | DDC [Fic]--dc23
LC record available at https://lccn.loc.gov/2018033686

Printed and bound in the United States of America.
VP 10 9 8 7 6 5 4 3 2 1

ONE

It's Thursday, and I haven't followed anybody all week. That's a long time for me. But with the school day over, the urge is strong as everyone leaves and heads home. I'm keeping my antennae up, just in case somebody catches my attention.

But I promised Charlie I wouldn't. Told her I'd go the whole week without doing it. Nobody stands out, anyway. I'll go home; my uncle won't be back from work for a few hours. I could get started on homework. I have a report due in a week that I keep putting off.

The gym door opens, and out storms Greg Matthes looking pissed. Really pissed. Which is news in and of itself. Look up *perfect* in the dictionary, and you'll find Greg's face grinning back at you. Seventeen, a senior, and a year ahead of me, popular, multiple-sport athlete Greg Matthes has a smile for everybody; it doesn't matter if you're a friend, teammate, acquaintance, or someone he just passes in the hall.

The reason Greg is angry could be big. Really big. If I'm going to be a detective or private investigator someday, I need to keep my skills sharp. I need to keep practicing. I shouldn't let this opportunity slip by.

Greg doesn't see me as he hoists his backpack—adorned in the school colors of orange and black, and covered with patches announcing every school sport he plays and every year he's played them—onto his back and strides purposefully away from the school. Shouldn't he have baseball practice now? An unzipped tan jacket covers the shirt baseball players usually wear for practice. Maybe he got thrown off the team. That would be big! My notebook is in my backpack, and I pull it out just in case I need to take notes.

In my head, Charlie's voice scolds me—*You promised, Alden*—and I hesitate. Another voice assures me—*She'll understand*. After allowing him a little distance, I start to tail him. I need to keep the right distance: not too close that he can sense me behind him, but not so far I could lose him. Fortunately, he never looks back. We go on that way for a while, and I have to work to keep up with him. But I'm skinny and wiry, and I walk a lot, so it's not a problem.

All of a sudden, he stops to pull out his phone. It must have rung, and I just didn't hear it. If I was closer, I'd need to slow down and walk nonchalantly past him so as not to look suspicious. Then I could pick him up again later. But I'm far enough back that I'm not going to pass him. Instead, I open my notebook to make it look like

I'm studying it and turn down a side street Greg has already passed. I keep going until I reach trees, my head and my eyes up.

He's half turned toward me, but isn't looking my way. He listens, then barks a few words into his cell I'm too far away to make out. He listens again, barks again, then angrily stuffs his cell back into his pocket. I pull back, but he turns away. Could the call have something to do with why he's angry? Maybe the call came from his girlfriend. She would normally be watching Greg at practice. I guess not this time. A rift between Greg Matthes and Amy Sloan would be bigger than Greg getting kicked off the baseball team.

If Greg's photo is next to perfect, Amy Sloan's would accompany *sweet* or *innocent*. Also a year ahead of me, she's one of the prettiest girls in school. I've found myself staring at her more than once. And while she's not a Jesus freak who goes out of her way to convert everyone she talks to, she makes it pretty clear the silver cross she wears around her neck is more than just jewelry. If Greg hopes for anything more than a kiss from her, he's going to have to wait until after marriage, I'm sure.

Which seems fine with Greg, far as I can tell. One time I had him on my list and followed him, figuring anyone who seems that perfect had to have secrets. Secrets that a good investigator should be able to uncover. But I ended up spending the entire time bored out of my mind. No matter when I followed him, after or before school or on the weekend, he'd always end up with Amy somewhere along the way. They'd meet with friends at McDonald's, Hardee's, the mall, or they'd just hang out together, always holding hands as if letting go might cause the world to explode. The one time they went to her house, Amy's mother was there to greet them. I'm sure she had chocolate chip cookies and milk ready. And they probably sat with just the right amount of space between them on the sofa while watching TV. After a week, I'd had enough. I decided they were as boring as they looked.

But maybe I was wrong. He starts moving again, and again I follow him, keeping pace. If he's on his way to see Amy, it's not at her house; he goes right by there without stopping. No cookies for Greggie today.

His house is just a couple of blocks farther, but he passes that as well, not even bothering to go inside to drop off his backpack.

We reach Fast Food Row, with one greasy franchise after another, but none of them interest Greg. And now we're leaving the places where Milton High kids tend to hang out and are entering territory I'm not as familiar with. We're approaching the edge of town, passing stretches of empty lots, a few lonely businesses, and the occasional abandoned building or three. With nobody else in sight for blocks, I give him more space, ready to duck behind a structure should he start to look back. There's been talk of renovating this part of Milton for the last few years, but nobody has gotten around to doing it. Why would Greg be walking here?

Maybe he doesn't have a destination in mind. Maybe that phone call made him so mad he just needed to walk off his anger, though it clearly hasn't worked.

Greg stops so abruptly I'm worried he's seen me. I hide behind the nearest building. He's looking in my direction now, and I prepare to run around to the other side of the building if he starts toward me. But after a few seconds, he looks the other way. Like he's looking for something. Or someone. Someone he's meeting? Who could be meeting him way out here?

All kinds of possibilities run through my mind. He's here to buy drugs. He's an athlete, so maybe it's steroids, and he comes all the way out here so no one he knows will see him. Or it could be worse than steroids. Could perfect Greg Matthes be a secret drug addict?

He's standing in front of what used to be Miller's Park, an abandoned Little League field that was torn down several years ago, after the newer, more modern park was built across town.

I'm not tall, I don't carry extra weight, and I do walk a lot, but following Greg all the way here at the pace he set has left me out of breath. But now that we're stopped, Greg looks more winded than I am. His perfect blond hair is plastered to his forehead and sweat shows on his muscular arms and legs, I can see wet spots on his shirt, and yet he looks like a model in a TV commercial. Meanwhile, I'm sure my sweaty stick arms, skinny legs, and damp T-shirt make me look like I'm in need of CPR.

Still, he shouldn't be *that* out of breath. Unless he's like this because of what's bothering him. Right now he looks more worried than angry.

He stands there for another minute, still glancing around. Then, taking one more deep breath, he turns and walks into the old park.

After letting him disappear, I cautiously follow. Once I see what's inside, I realize how hard it will be to stay hidden.

There are two fields, both barren and clearly in disrepair. The closer field still has part of its backstop behind what used to be home plate, though the metal is bent and rusty. Two splintered benches where the players used to sit also remain, as do a set of bleachers on the third-base side of the field. What's left of the basepaths is packed dirt, littered with stones and trash; the outfield is weedy and overgrown.

The second field is farther back and in worse shape. There are no bleachers or backstop and only the barest outline of basepaths. All that remains is the brick structure I think was once a dugout, though the bench for the players to sit on is gone.

Greg's back is to me, and I quickly run to the bleachers. Crouching down behind them, I slide off my backpack and peer out.

He's headed toward the other field. But someone is waiting. Female. Standing near what used to be first base. It's a distance, but I'd know Amy's bright-red hair and the blue jacket anywhere.

Did she see me coming in behind her boyfriend? I remain crouched behind the bleachers, ready to run at the first sign I've been compromised. But her attention seems focused on Greg as he approaches her.

This makes no sense. Why meet all the way out here? It can't be for anything good. Maybe that's what Greg's angry phone conversation was about. Amy checking to make sure he was on his way? He sure didn't seem happy to be reminded.

I wish I were closer. Sometimes I carry binoculars with me, but I don't have them now. I consider running to the backstop; it won't hide me as well as the bleachers, but I could get a closer look. I start to stand up, then change my mind. Too risky. At least they're far enough away they shouldn't be able to see me, as long as I'm careful.

As soon as Greg reaches her, Amy wraps her arms around him. She tries to kiss him, but Greg forces her to let go. Uh-oh. Trouble in paradise? First Greg says something, then Amy. I can't hear either of them, but I still pull out my notebook and a pen and start taking notes.

They're gesturing at each other. Both upset about something. This is no ordinary fight. This could be them breaking up. It wouldn't be long before the word was out at school: the dream couple together no more. And I would be the first to know about it.

Their voices rise as they yell back and forth. All I'm getting are fragments.

"You have to!" Amy shouts. Her voice is higher pitched than normal.

Greg comes back with, "No! You can't make me…" The rest is unintelligible.

Then Amy: "…you don't, I'm going to…" It fades away again.

Greg: "No! Let's talk about this…"

Amy brusquely starts walking away from him, toward the dugout. He follows her, shouting, "Don't you walk away from…" He grabs her by the arm to turn her around, but she resists, pulling away so hard she stumbles. Greg tries to help but she shakes him off.

"Don't touch me!"

Greg says something I don't hear. Amy follows with, "Leave me alone!" then marches away, disappearing behind the brick wall. Greg pushes off his backpack as he, too, disappears behind the wall.

I wait for them to reappear. Except they don't. I hear nothing.

A full minute goes by. Nothing. I'm not sure what to do. Maybe instead of walking along the wall, they're walking away from the wall, which is why I can't see them. They could be getting away.

I creep out from behind the bleachers, ready to jump back behind them if necessary. I can't see anything, so I inch sideways, slowly, carefully, trying to find the right angle to see behind the wall while still keeping out of sight.

This is ridiculous. They could be making out back there. Though, knowing Amy, I kind of doubt it. Still, I should just leave.

I start to turn away, but something makes me stop. A sound of some kind. A voice, maybe, blurting out "No!" or "Don't!" Maybe.

And then, I see movement. Something flying up high above the wall before descending out of sight. It happens so quickly I can't tell for sure what I saw. There's a thud. I can't think of what else to call it. Then something else. Not loud but it could have been somebody crying out. In pain.

Followed by silence.

My chest hurts; I've been holding my breath. I let it out and keep moving. I have to make sure there's nothing wrong. I'm past the backstop now and still don't see anything. I keep going. There's nothing protecting me now. Any second Greg and Amy could reappear from behind the wall, and I'd be caught, stuck with having to explain what I'm doing here.

But the hard knot in my stomach will only be untied by me seeing for sure what's going on back there.

I'll just take a quick peek. Then I'll leave.

Only a few more steps...

My heart stops as Greg reappears, holding his backpack by the straps. Is that... Is that blood on it? He's crouching down; there's something lying on the ground at his feet. It takes me a moment to realize what I'm seeing.

I cry out. How loud, I'm not sure.

And then I'm running, out of the park, down the sidewalk.

Do I hear footsteps? I don't dare look back. I just keep running, and I don't stop running until I'm pounding on my best friend's front door.

TWO

"What did you see?" Charlie asks. I could barely talk when she first opened the door, out of breath, with a huge weight pushing against my chest and a sharp pain ripping through my left side. Charlie's the same age as me, but a lot stronger from her after-school weightlifting sessions. So when I'd started to collapse she caught me easily, brought me inside, guided me to the living room couch, and got me water to drink. Her parents aren't home yet, which I knew. Her mom works in an office, her dad is the chief of police. Charlie and I have been friends since forever.

I'm taking another sip of water, and Charlie asks me again, "What did you see?"

"A body," I blurt out.

"A what?"

"A body."

"You're sure?"

"No, I made it up!"

"Alden, this is not a game!"

"Do I *sound* like I'm playing a game?"

Charlie says nothing.

"It was Amy. Lying on the ground. At Greg's feet." I take a breath. "I think she was dead."

Charlie stands up from the couch. "Why do you think she was dead?"

"She wasn't moving. Or breathing."

"How can you be sure? You said it was a distance. Maybe you just couldn't tell."

"Greg was holding his backpack. It looked heavy, like it was filled with a ton of books. He must have hit her with it. Swung it like a sledgehammer. I think there was…blood…on it."

"You *think*."

I stare at her. "There was blood."

Charlie stares back at me, then walks a couple of steps. She turns back to me. "She might have been dead," she says. "Or she could have been unconscious. Or even awake. You don't know. You didn't check her."

"How could I check her? Greg was right there."

"Did you call the police?"

"No, I…I just ran."

"Did he see you?"

"I don't think so."

"You don't *think* so?"

"I'm not sure, okay? I was too busy running. I…" I look down, ashamed. "I panicked, okay? I'm sorry. Maybe he saw me. I don't know."

Charlie stares at me, thinking. When she's quiet like this, I know it's best to stay silent. Charlise Walker—everybody calls her Charlie—can be intimidating, with her buzz cut, muscular arms, and eyebrow piercings, a small stud on each one. She had to prove to her dad she could get a C in math for one grading period before he let her do it.

Charlie is stronger than 90 percent of the students at Milton High, not to mention taller. We are a pair of opposites, dark and light, strong and scrawny, though at five feet nine I still have hope I might one day catch up to her six feet. I don't know what drew us together, I just know she's always been there, both while growing up and after my parents were killed last summer.

The way she's looking at me reminds me of her father. Matt Walker is a solid guy, firm but fair. After my parents died, he and his wife took me in until my uncle came forward. Charlie's dad takes being a cop very seriously, so she's never told him about my predilection for following people. He wouldn't like it, nor would he be pleased to learn his daughter has kept it from him. But she keeps my secret, just like I'd keep hers—if she ever had any.

I look down at my hands. After another minute, Charlie crosses to the couch and puts her hand on my shoulder. "You were right to run," she says. "If Greg really hurt her or…worse, who knows what he might have done to you. But you need to call the police."

I start to pull out my phone, but I hesitate. "Do I have to use my cell?"

"You want to place the call anonymously?"

"If I leave my name, it means getting involved—"

She looks at me. "You're already involved! What happened to *not* following anybody for a little while?"

I don't say anything, guilt and anxiety battling for supremacy. Charlie sighs. "My dad may be suspicious after getting burned by those other prank calls the past several months. But if this really happened—"

"What do you mean *if*?"

"If she needs help," Charlie says, talking over me, "the police need to get there. Right away. If you need to, you can give them your name later."

"Sound goods," I say.

"I still think there's a pay phone a couple of blocks down and one street over. We'll use that. If you don't give your name and the police just track it to a phone booth, it won't matter."

"Okay," I say.

"Let's go," Charlie orders.

As we're about to leave, I ask Charlie, "You believe me, don't you?"

The flash of doubt I see in her eyes is gone before she says, "Yes."

We hurry outside. After reaching the phone booth I realize I have no change. "You're calling 911, dummy," Charlie says. "You don't need any." Her teasing smile helps me relax a little.

I don't see anybody on either side of the street as I place the call. No passing cars, either. I can't speak to who might be home, though, looking out their front window.

I dial 911 and wait until someone answers. I keep the call short. To the point.

"Two people were fighting. At the old Miller's Park. I think a girl's been killed." I hang up, out of breath.

"Did you have to say 'killed?'"

"I…"

"You could have just said she was hurt."

"Maybe *you* should have called," I tell her.

"And you didn't say a name."

"The plan was not to give my—"

"Amy's name. Greg's."

"You think I should've?"

"I don't know," Charlie says after a moment. She looks around. "Let's get out of here."

We hurry back to Charlie's house without trying to look like we're hurrying. Once inside, I collapse back onto her couch. "Now what?" I manage to say.

"Go home."

"Home?" I ask as if I've never heard the word before.

"Yes," she answers. "And just act normal."

"Why can't I be normal here?"

She thinks about it. "No. If the police do figure the call came from that phone booth, better you weren't here."

"Normal," I say. "I can do that." Then I look at Charlie. "How are we gonna know? Will you ask your dad about it when he gets home?"

"I can't just ask him, that'd look suspicious. But if something's really happened to Amy, Dad'll be talking about it. I'll call you later tonight."

"Okay." I hesitate though, then say, "I'm sorry."

"For what?"

"For getting you into this."

"What are friends for?" she says. "Don't worry about it. You did the right thing, calling."

I nod. "And I'm sorry for lying."

Her brow furrows. "Lying?"

"Telling you I was going to stop following people."

"If the police get there in time, you following Greg might have saved Amy's life."

I hadn't thought of that. For some reason, it doesn't make me feel any better.

As I'm about to walk out the door, Charlie stops me and asks, "Did you take any notes about what you saw yet?"

The question surprises me. She's never asked me about this before. "No," I say. "Well, just a few notes before I ran."

"Don't write anymore," she says. "Rip out the page with the notes and hide it."

"Hide it?"

"Yes."

"Why?"

"If it's nothing, you can burn it later so nobody knows it was you who made the call. If it's something, you don't want to—"

There's that word *if* again. "Want to what?"

"Just do what I say. Please."

"Okay," I say after a moment, a little angry she still has doubts.

Walking home, though, I can't help but feel like *I'm* being followed.

THREE

Charlie may not like me following people, but at least she knows why I do it.

It's hard to stop. People are strange. I learn a lot.

And if I'd been as observant last summer as I am now, my parents might still be alive.

I'm always watching, listening. If someone becomes interesting enough, I add him or her to my list of people to follow.

Following is fascinating and daring and sometimes a little dangerous. But I have to do it. It's important work. You never know about people; what they show on the outside is often not what's on the inside. You've gotta watch for those brief moments when the hidden part slips out.

Studying people so I can understand what makes them tick is a good skill to have if I really am going to be an investigator. So what I'm doing now? It's all just practice.

The tricks I've picked up following people worked for me while I was trailing Greg. But, really, following is easier than you might think. People are oblivious, too caught up in their own stuff to pay attention to what's around them. It makes it easy for me not to be noticed.

It's how I learned my science teacher is dating my gym teacher, though they go out of their way to hide it from everyone in school, and how I found out Milton bad boy Steve Latimer, who spends more time in detention than he does in class, finds time two after-noons a week to volunteer at a day care for kids with special needs. And I discovered that Rick Kellerman, star of the school's wrestling team, is really into fashion magazines.

It's amazing the things I learn. People and their secrets.

Despite what Charlie recommended, I finish my notes after I get home. Not doing it feels dishonest somehow. They'll be safe. I always keep my notebook close by. Nobody's ever going to read it but me.

By the time my uncle gets home from work, I'm almost finished with my homework. Uncle Bill works construction, does a lot of overtime, and he's always bone-tired when he gets home. He's a nice guy; he didn't have to uproot his life to become my guardian, move to Milton, and get a new job so I could keep living here. For someone who was never married or had kids of his own, and who suddenly became responsible for taking care of a teenager, he does okay. But he's not much for long conversations. He'll ask me the usual questions: "How was school?" or "Got any homework? Need any help with it?"

I'll fill him in on basic stuff about the school day, and when I tell him I don't need help with homework, he always seems grateful. Once dinner is over, not long after he's planted himself in his armchair in front of the TV, beer in hand, he'll be out like a light. At some point, he'll wake up and get himself upstairs to bed, but I'm usually long asleep before that happens.

He's not mean and never gets angry. I get good grades, and whenever I come home with another A on a paper or test, he'll tell me how smart he thinks I am, just like my dad. Hearing him mention either of my parents makes my heart ache.

We don't usually talk about them, my mom and dad. Though lately he's been bringing them up more and more, especially Dad. There have been times when, on the nights he's had an extra beer or two, I'll hear him mumbling to himself. And I'll hear my dad's name.

Reminding me he must miss him, too.

The early evening news has nothing about a body found in old Miller's Park. Dinner tonight is chili, one of about six meals my uncle knows how to make. I like his chili, but my stomach is too tied up to eat. He's not too tired to notice.

"You're not eating," he says. "Are you all right?"

"I'm fine." I manage to wolf down enough spoonfuls to satisfy him. I think he might say something more, but he just returns to his food, and we both go back to a quiet meal.

Later, I'm in my room upstairs, finishing up what's left of my homework, when my cell phone rings.

Charlie.

I don't even say hi. "What'd you hear?"

"Nothing."

"Your father didn't talk about it?"

"Oh, he talked about it," she says. "A lot. I mean they found *nothing* at Miller's Park. No Amy, no Greg, no sign of a fight, nothing. He spent half of dinner complaining about kids that make prank calls to the station. Three now in the past ten months. The other two were bad enough, claiming someone had a gun. But this one he called particularly bad because the caller claimed someone might have been killed. My dad says he's not going to let this one slide. He's going to find the kid who did it."

"I shouldn't have called. I should have just—"

"You were right to call," Charlie says. "You did the right thing."

"But your dad—"

"Relax. He's just blowing off steam. They don't know where the call came from. They're not going to find you."

"What if someone saw us in the phone booth?"

"Take some deep breaths, Alden."

I take two deep breaths, but they don't do much to settle the fluttering in my chest.

"This isn't a TV show where they trace the call before the

commercial," Charlie continues. "Our little community police department isn't big enough to track down one phone booth. There'll be the article in the paper tomorrow, then things will die down. Don't worry. Besides, this is good news."

"Good news…"

"This means Amy's alive. She just fell or something. That's probably why you saw her lying on the ground."

I say nothing.

"Or they were making out together on the grass," she continues, "and when you saw them, Greg had just gotten up. If you'd stayed a little longer you probably would have seen Amy get up, too."

She pauses.

"Alden? You there?"

"He could have moved Amy's body," I say.

"Jeez, Alden. Greg Matthes isn't some criminal mastermind. And besides, you told me he walked there, didn't have a car. You think he dragged her somewhere? No way."

After a few seconds, I say, "I guess you're right."

"You bet I am. Tomorrow you're going to school, and you'll see Amy there. Then you're going to breathe a big sigh of relief, and everything will get back to normal."

Another deep breath. "Okay."

"And then you're going to stop following people."

I don't respond.

"It's creepy," she says.

I still don't respond.

"Promise me you're going to stop following people, Alden. And mean it this time."

Silence.

Then I let out a big sigh. "Okay."

"Promise?"

Another sigh. "Promise."

"Okay." Then she adds, "You big goof."

"You're bigger than I am."

"Bigger and stronger. But not goofier."

We both laugh. This is a familiar refrain between us. I'm sure most people would think it sounds dumb, but we've said it for years.

"Good night, Alden."

"Good night."

Charlie ends the call.

She has a way of making me feel better when something's bothering me. I like to think the rare smile she reserves for me is not one she shares with others.

As I try to drift off to sleep, I tell myself she's right. I'll go to school tomorrow, and Amy will be there.

Except what if she isn't?

FOUR

Uncle Bill is up drinking coffee and reading the newspaper as usual when I come downstairs in the morning. "Breakfast is on the stove," he says in his gruff voice, over the edge of his paper.

I expect my uncle to just go back to what he's doing like he did the night before, but to my surprise, his eyes stay on me as I walk over to the stove. "You're not coming down with something, are you?" he asks. "You don't look good."

I must really look like crap if I'm keeping him from reading his paper. "I'm fine." I make sure to smile. "I was just up later than I thought I'd be, doing homework."

"Do you need to stay home? I can write you a note. Nothing wrong with a day off every now and then."

"My homework's due today. And I...I have a test." I try to remember if I actually do.

Uncle Bill grins. "When we were kids, your dad liked to try and talk Mom and Dad into giving him a day off. It never worked."

There it is again—bringing up my dad out of nowhere. Does he expect me to respond? My heart suddenly pounding into my throat, I turn to the stove and serve myself some eggs and bacon.

He returns to his paper.

I force down the food to hold off any more questions. My uncle points to the front page and says, "It says here somebody called the police, claimed a girl was killed."

My heart leaps into my throat, and I almost choke on my eggs.

Uncle Bill doesn't seem to notice as he continues. "It says when the police got there, there was nothing. No body. It was a prank call. Did you hear about this?"

I carefully wipe my mouth. "Uh…no."

"Well, the police chief sounds pretty upset. He'll probably find out who did it." He puts the paper down and checks his watch. "Gotta go," he says. "Have a good day at school, Alden."

As soon as the door closes behind him, I grab the paper and pore over the article. Charlie's dad does seem pissed. He's quoted as calling it "reprehensible," and mentions other prank calls made in the past. Then he goes on to say, "I promise we will do our best to track down the people responsible and make sure they are arrested and punished to the full extent of the law."

For someone whose department supposedly doesn't have the tools to track me down, he sure sounds determined. I expect police cruisers to drive up to me any minute, sirens blaring, as I walk to school.

• • •

At school, Amy is a no-show. Every worst-case scenario plays over and over in my mind. I'm practically jumping out of my skin by the time I see Charlie at lunch.

"Yeah I know. Amy's not here," Charlie says before I even open my mouth. "She's at church camp."

"Church camp? How do you know?"

"I know people who know Amy," she says.

"You asked around?"

"Don't worry, I was subtle. I can be subtle, you know."

Charlie is friends with the jocks who use the weight room. It makes sense she would know a lot of the same kids Greg does, though Charlie doesn't play any sports. What doesn't make sense to most of my classmates is her friendship with me.

"It's a three-day camp," Charlie continues. "She got today off from school so she could go."

"How do we know she's really there?"

"What do you mean?"

"Maybe she never made it to camp. Her friends think that's where she is, so no one's suspicious. It gives Greg plenty of time to get rid of her body and any evidence."

Charlie gives me a funny look. "Greg's in school today, you know. Don't you think he'd at least call in sick if he needed to get rid of a body?"

The sarcasm in her voice is obvious, so I don't bother answering.

"I told you, Alden, this isn't a TV show. Besides, don't you think her parents would notice her missing and report it to the police?"

"Unless they think she's at camp, too."

"And how would that work?" Charlie scowls. "You're not making sense."

I open my mouth, then close it. I decide to change course. "I've been keeping my eye on Greg."

Charlie's scowl deepens. "What do you mean keeping an eye on him?"

"Not following him. Just…watching him when I see him in the hall."

Charlie starts to say something, then stops and shrugs. "So?"

"He doesn't seem himself today."

"Oh, really."

"You know how he is. Smiling all the time. Always friendly."

"All that to hide the fact that he's really a vicious killer." Charlie wiggles her fingers in front of her face while singing the beginning of the theme from *The Twilight Zone*. A year ago the two of us binged the entire series during spring break. We loved it.

"He's just not himself, Charlie. He's quiet, sullen."

"Maybe he misses Amy."

"I thought I caught him looking at me a couple of times in the hall."

"So?"

"It might be because he saw me running away at Miller's Park."

"But you weren't sure he even saw you, right?"

"Well…yeah. I mean, no, I'm not sure he saw me."

"You're not sure about a lot of things."

"But, Charlie…"

"Yes?"

"He doesn't have his backpack today."

Charlie blinks.

"He always has it at school," I continue. "With all that sports stuff on it. He had it yesterday when I was following him. But not today."

After a few seconds, Charlie asks, "What's he carrying today?"

"An old gray one."

"It doesn't mean—"

"I told you what I saw at the park."

"What you *thought* you saw."

I lean in. "If he killed Amy with it, it might have her blood on it. I thought I *saw* blood on it. Which is why he couldn't bring it to school today."

"Maybe he just broke a strap."

I glare at her in silence.

"I'm going to regret this," she says, shaking her head. "What do you want to do?"

"Come with me to Miller's Park. Help me look for evidence."

"Evidence? The police were there, don't you think they would have found something?"

"They expected to find a body. When they didn't and figured they just got pranked, they probably didn't look too hard."

"You don't know that."

"Charlie, it wouldn't hurt just to take a look."

"The police might still be keeping an eye on the park, you know."

"Why would they if they didn't find anything the first time? If we see a police car, we'll just leave." I give her my best imploring look. I can tell she's wavering.

"What evidence do you think we'll find?"

"I don't know. Blood on the grass. Or somewhere. Maybe we'll find Greg's backpack. He might have left it there or threw it in a trash can."

"That'd be pretty dumb of him," Charlie says. She goes silent. I know to wait and keep my mouth shut as she thinks about it.

Finally, she says, "All right. We'll do it. After school. Let's go to my house, we'll use my bikes. If we get there and see a police car, we won't stop. We'll just keep going, and we'll forget about it. Clear?"

"Clear," I say.

FIVE

After lunch, I see Greg a few times in the hall. He doesn't look my way either time. Meeting Charlie after school, she says, "You know, we could just call her house."

I'm too busy looking for Greg among the crowd of departing students to respond right away. I don't see him, which means he probably has baseball practice today.

"Earth to Alden."

"What?" I say, looking at her. "Call her house?"

"Sure," Charlie says. "I call, ask for Amy. If one of her parents answers and tells me she's not there because she's away at camp for the weekend, I'll ask for her cell number, claim I need to ask her about a homework assignment or something. I'll call her cell, Amy will answer, I'll hang up, and we're good. We don't have to go look for 'evidence.'" She used air quotes for "evidence."

I put my hand on her wrist as she takes out her phone. "Shouldn't you use the phone booth?"

"To call her mom?" Charlie says. "Nah. Let's live dangerously." She dials for information, asks for Sloan on Grantham Street. She hits the speakerphone so I can hear as the operator places the call.

A female voice picks up. "Hello?"

"May I speak to Amy, please?" Charlie asks, putting on an extra sweet voice.

"She's not here," the voice responds.

"Oh. Do you know when she'll be home?"

"I'm afraid she's gone for the weekend at a camp. May I take a message? She'll be home Sunday night."

Charlie gives me a knowing smirk. "Would you mind giving me Amy's cell phone number?"

"I understand they don't allow cell phones at the camp."

"I really need to talk to her about an important class assignment, Mrs. Sloan."

"Oh, I'm not Mrs. Sloan. Did you need to speak to her?"

Charlie hesitates. "Sure," she says, shrugging her shoulders at me. I shrug, too, though I feel nervous as hell.

"Oh, I'm sorry," the voice says. "I should have said if you want to speak to Mrs. Sloan, I'll need to take a message, too. She and Mr. Sloan don't return from their trip until Monday afternoon."

My heart seems to stop. Charlie says, "Trip?"

"They've been out of town since Wednesday. Amy left last night or this morning, I'm not sure which. I'm house-sitting and just got here this afternoon. I can take a message for either one of them."

"No, that's all right. I'll see Amy at school on Monday."

"Maybe I should take your name—"

"Thanks so much," Charlie says quickly and hangs up.

We stare at each other. Ultimately, I break the silence. "Amy's parents have been gone since before she was supposed to leave. Before I saw Greg...do what he did."

Charlie doesn't respond.

"Which means they wouldn't know something's happened to her. They think she's at church camp."

"Oh, come on. You don't think they'd have called her when she was about to leave, to say goodbye?"

I dig in. "Maybe they couldn't. So they called her Wednesday night or Thursday morning to say bye."

Charlie digs in, too. "Or had her call when she got to camp? To make sure she got there okay?"

"The house sitter said cell phones weren't allowed."

"There must be some kind of phone at the place. She still could have called."

"Maybe," I say. "But with what I saw at the park yesterday, even you have to admit this is suspicious."

Charlie opens her mouth, then closes it.

We stand together in silence. It's a pretty warm day, but I feel a deep chill go through me.

"All right," Charlie finally says. "Let's go to Miller's Park. See what we can find."

We walk to her house and go inside just long enough to drop off our books. Then, pulling out Charlie's two bicycles, we take off.

SIX

Miller's Park looks the same as it did yester-
day. Abandoned. Beat up. Like no one has been here in a long time.
There are no police cars in sight, so we wheel our bikes inside.

A trash can sits near the entrance. Not a lot of garbage in there,
so it takes me less than a minute to go through it. "No backpack,"
I announce.

Charlie puts a hand above her eyes to block the sunlight as she
peers out. "Where did you see Greg and Amy?"

I point. "At the other field. Near first base. Then they walked
over behind that dugout wall."

"And where were you?"

"Behind these bleachers."

"That's pretty far," Charlie says. "Okay, let's split up. You take
one side of the park, and I'll take the other. See if one of us finds
the backpack. Though, like I said, he'd be stupid to leave it here."

"Maybe we'll find some other clue."

Charlie shrugs, and we begin our search, taking a good twenty minutes to scour the park. Nothing. I find another trash can, but it's empty. No trash or a backpack. I check behind and under bushes and the edge of the outfield by the far fence. Again, nothing. Frustrated, I meet Charlie back where we started.

"I'll stand here behind the bleachers," she says. "You go to where they were standing while you were watching them."

I trot out to the second field and stand on first base. Charlie's disappeared behind the bleachers.

My phone rings just as she reappears, her cell to her ear. "Why are you calling me?" I ask.

"You're pretty far out there," she says from my phone. "I'm not going to yell. Walk to the wall, go behind it, then come back out." I do as she asks, waiting a couple of seconds before stepping out again. While Charlie heads toward me, I start to check the ground behind the wall.

"I looked there already," she says when she reaches me. "No backpack and no blood, either." She glances toward the bleachers. "That's a good distance. Where was she lying on the ground?"

I move to the spot. "About here."

"And where were you when you saw her?"

Pointing, I say, "Over there on the other field, a little past the backstop. I was trying to get a better angle."

"That's pretty far, too," Charlie says. "And you only saw her for a few seconds, right?"

I nod.

"Okay. Walk to where you were standing when you saw her."

I jog to the backstop then walk past it until I'm at the same angle as yesterday. We never hung up, so I put the phone to my ear. "I was about here," I say.

"Good," Charlie responds. "I'm going to lie down on my stomach. After I do, watch me for fifteen seconds. Then come back and tell me whether I was holding my breath or breathing. You got it?"

"Got it," I say.

I set my cell's timer for fifteen seconds while Charlie lays on the ground. "This about right?" she asks from my cell.

"Yes."

I start the timer, watching Charlie intently until the alarm goes off. Then I run to the wall. Charlie is on her feet by the time I get there.

"Well?" she says. "Which was it?"

To be honest, I'm not sure. So I guess. "You were holding your breath."

"Nope. I was breathing the whole time."

"Maybe we should try it again."

"How about we don't," Charlie says. "Hey, don't look so

unhappy. It's good news we didn't find anything. It means you were probably wrong. Whatever it was you saw, it wasn't Amy lying dead on the ground. Besides, if she really didn't show up at camp, don't you think the people in charge there would have called her parents, and they'd be home looking for her? Face it, Alden, she's at camp having fun with the other Jesus freaks."

"Don't call her that," I hear myself say.

"Sorry. I mean other God-fearing, religious teenagers."

"Cut it out."

"Why? You have a crush on Amy?"

Heat spreads across my face as I turn away and start examining the grass behind the wall.

"Wait a minute. *Do* you have a crush on Amy?" Charlie asks.

"Let's look some more…" I keep checking the grass.

"I never thought of you as being interested in the religious type." Her tone softens. "Amy is a nice girl, though. Too nice, in my opinion. But if you…" She stops. I'm still not looking at her. "What are you doing?" she asks.

"Looking for blood," I say.

"I told you, I looked here already."

"Did you check the wall?"

"Check the wall?"

"Look here." I point to a copper-colored spot more than halfway up the wall about the size of a quarter. "That could be blood."

Charlie moves in for a closer look. "It could be anything."

"When Greg hit Amy with his backpack, she might have hit her head against the wall before she fell. Then some of the blood got on the backpack."

Charlie peers closely at it for several seconds. "Maybe," she says. "A big maybe."

I refuse to give up. "We should keep looking in case we missed something."

"We didn't miss anything, Alden. It's time to go." When I don't say anything, she sighs. "Monday'll get here, Amy will be back from camp, and everything will go back to normal."

"All right," I say, my shoulders slumping. "I guess you're right."

"I'm always right," she announces, taking a step.

She stops. Looks down.

"What?" I ask.

"I think I stepped on some…" She crouches down to the grass and comes back up scrutinizing something in her hand. Wordlessly, she gives it to me.

I recognize it immediately. A silver cross, beautifully ornate, dangles on the end of a chain. I've seen it before, many times. Every day at school, in fact. If it isn't hanging from Amy's neck, she's playing with it, rubbing the cross between her fingers as she walks between classes. She may not even know she does it. But I know. I'm guessing the whole school knows.

"Read the back," I hear Charlie say.

Turning the cross over, I find engraved words: *To Amy. Love Mom and Dad.*

"It proves she was here," I mutter. "Look, the clasp is broken. What if it fell off when she…" When she what? Tripped and fell to the ground? Was making out with Greg? Or when Greg hit her with his backpack?

Charlie's voice is soft as she says, "She's supposed to be at church camp."

I look up. Her gaze is still on the cross in my hand. "So?"

"She loves that cross," Charlie says. "I've never seen her without it. She probably sleeps with it." Her eyes dark and intense. "No way would she go to church camp without it."

"It could be all right. If she lost it—" I start, realizing I've suddenly become Charlie and she's become me.

Charlie interrupts with a shake of her head. "A friend of mine told me about how one time Amy jumped up from her desk right in the middle of Mr. Talbot's lecture, all frantic because she'd realized her cross wasn't around her neck," she says. "She insisted she *had* to find it, got Mr. Talbot and the whole class searching everywhere in the classroom for it. It turned out it was on the floor just inside the door. She was so relieved she actually cried. Believe me, she'd have been back here looking for it. And she would've remembered she was behind this wall with Greg. We found it just by chance. Amy would have combed every inch of this spot, the whole park if necessary. She would have found it."

Now we're both looking at the cross again. Charlie says, "The only way she isn't wearing this…"

I finish for her. "…is if she's dead."

SEVEN

Last summer, on the day my parents were killed, I remember how loud the siren was inside the police car, blasting at me from all sides.

A police officer sat in the back seat with her arm around me, while Charlie's father drove as fast as he could. Being the chief of police, he probably should have stayed behind at Milton Park to deal with the shooting's aftermath; my parents were only two of six people shot that day. But he was there, rushing me to the hospital, just a few minutes behind the two ambulances that carried my mother and father.

The officer next to me was talking, but I couldn't hear her over the siren's scream. Chief Walker seemed to say something every now and then as well, but I couldn't hear him, either.

It didn't matter, though. I didn't need to hear them say, "It's going to be all right," when I knew it wasn't true. I had seen my parents lying on the grass together, in their own pools of blood before the paramedics arrived and took them away.

When we got to the hospital, a doctor took us into another room. I didn't need her to tell me that my father had died on the way in the ambulance, and that my mother had made it into the hospital before she died.

I already knew they were both dead.

And that things were never going to be all right again.

EIGHT

A good investigator always makes a plan.

Charlie and I hurry back to school to see if Greg is still at baseball practice. If we follow him, we might be able to learn something. Or maybe we'll find he never showed at all. That he bowed out, feigning sickness, so he could get rid of a body. But the team is already finished by the time we get there. No way to tell if Greg had ditched or not. We bike to his house, but no one seems home. A playground across the street makes it easier for us to look like two people just talking instead of keeping an eye on the Matthes house.

"Maybe we should see if he's at the mall," I say. "He might be there."

"He could be anywhere," Charlie points out.

"You go. I'll stay here in case he comes home. I'll text you if he does, or you can text me if you find him."

"What if he's not at the mall?"

"Check Fast Food Row. If you don't find him, just come back here. We'll wait for him."

"What if he's out till late? We have homework. You left your books at my house before we went to Miller's Field, remember? And your uncle and my parents might have something to say about coming home late without telling them where we were first."

"We'll call them, make up some excuse—"

"Alden, stop. Sit down. Take a breath."

I start to say more, but she gives me that hard stare of hers. I shut up and sit on a nearby bench, taking deep breaths. After a moment, her gaze softens, and she sits down next to me. "Maybe we should call the police," she says. "Talk to my dad."

"And tell him what?" I say. "That we found Amy's necklace at Miller's Park, so she must be dead?"

"You can tell him what you saw."

"He'll know I was the one who made that call. The one he thinks was a prank."

"You'll tell him it wasn't a prank. I'll be there to back you up."

"It'll piss him off," I argue, "especially if he finds out you were with me when I made the call and didn't tell him. You'll get in trouble, too."

"Let me worry about that."

"He'll never believe me."

"Why not?" Charlie says. "He knows you. He likes you. And like I said, I'll have your back."

"But you didn't see it happen," I say, feeling more agitated. "Only I did. It'll be like the last two times."

"What do you mean 'like the last two times?'"

Crap! Why did I say that?

Charlie stares at me. "Alden, what are you... Wait a minute. Are you talking about..."

I've never told Charlie it was me. I've never told anyone.

I tell her now.

The first time it happened was a few weeks after the shooting. I was living with the Walkers. The legal stuff was still being worked out so my uncle could become my guardian, and he was looking for a new job and closing the sale of his house so he could move to Milton.

I was at the mall with Charlie and her mom buying clothes for the coming school year. Mrs. Walker had given me some cash to spend, and I was in a store checking out shirts when I saw a man who looked suspicious. Following him, I swore I saw the outline of a gun pressed against his jacket pocket. After following him into a toy store filled with children, I went to the mall's nearest pay phone and called the police. I hung up without leaving my name. The town was still on edge over the shooting that had just killed my parents, so it didn't take long for the police to show up full force, Chief Walker in the forefront, to take him down. But all he had on him was a cell phone, a wallet with his ID, cash, and credit cards, and some loose change. And, in a bag, a Star Wars ship he had just bought for his kid. No gun. It turned out the guy was at the mall with his wife and son. The incident was a big story on the evening news and in the next morning's paper. It even got some national attention, considering what had happened in Milton at the summer fair. Fortunately, the guy didn't sue. He'd been at the fair himself that day, he said, and he understood.

The second time was a month into the new school year. Uncle Bill had been living with me about five weeks when I swore I saw Gavin Mackee carrying a gun into school. I kept my eye on him, this time waiting until I was sure I'd seen it on him a second time, before calling the police. Again, anonymously. The school went into full lockdown. Again, Chief Walker showed up with what seemed like the entire force.

They took all the students out of the building. Gavin swore he did not have a gun, but they searched him anyway, as well as his locker and his book bag. They even checked the entire school building, thinking he might have hidden it somewhere. No gun. It was a big news story then, too. Another example, the newscasts said, of a town still on edge after the horrible shooting that summer. I didn't tell anyone it was me. Not even Charlie.

Chief Walker was angry, of course. He swore he'd find out who made the two calls. Deep down, I was afraid he already knew. But he never said anything.

After that, I realized if I saw something suspicious in the future, I would need proof before calling the police, which meant I needed to improve my observation and investigation skills.

I went online and learned ways to follow people without being seen. Then I began practicing by picking people to follow. I took notes. Even collected evidence when I could, though it never came to anything.

Until I followed Greg Matthes to Miller's Park.

"That was you, both times?" Charlie says.

I nod.

"Gavin was messed up about that for a long time."

"I know," I say in a small voice. "I'm sorry. I really thought I saw…" I let my words trail off.

"Why didn't you tell me?" she asks.

"Your dad's the police chief."

"So you don't trust me?"

"That's not it. I didn't want to put you in a bad position."

Shaking her head, Charlie gets up from the bench and stands with her hands on her hips. I stare at the ground, saying nothing. We stay that way for a long time. Finally, she sits back down and says, "You have to tell my dad what you saw."

"You mean you believe me?" I ask, surprised. "After what I told you?"

"You're not the kind of person who plays pranks like that. I'm sure you thought you were doing the right thing. Even if you were wrong about the guns."

"You believe I saw Greg kill Amy?"

"There's a big difference between thinking you saw a gun and seeing somebody get murdered. The look on your face when you showed up at my house yesterday…that was real. And finding Amy's cross near where you said it happened…"

Finally, she looks at me. "Yes, Alden. I believe you."

Her words are reassuring.

"But you should tell my father."

"And if he figures out I was the one who made those other calls, which he will, he'll think this is a prank, too. He's already called it a prank in the newspaper."

"But you're talking about murder this time. A murder you saw."

"If I go to him without proof, he'll just think I'm crazy."

"Don't be ridiculous."

"I think he knows I made those calls. He probably already thinks I'm crazy."

"You know that's not true. My dad's been nothing but nice to you. He and Mom took you in—"

"I know. I'm grateful. I'm sorry." I close my eyes and take another deep breath.

Charlie breaks the silence. "Do you want to talk about it? You've never really talked about…you know."

I do know.

It happened so fast. My father shouting my name. Trying to protect me, just before the first gunshots rang out. My parents falling to the ground. Me falling, too. More gunshots. People screaming, running.

And I could have stopped it.

"Hey?"

Hearing Charlie's voice brings me back to the present.

"Are you all right?" she asks.

I hesitate, then nod.

"I'm sorry. I shouldn't have brought up—"

"No, *I'm* sorry," I say. "Your parents have been very kind to me. I don't know what I would have done without…"

Again, I hesitate. "I have to get it right this time." I look at her, trying to make her understand. "Especially if we're going to accuse one of the most popular students at Milton High of killing his girlfriend."

Charlie doesn't respond.

"We need more evidence."

"Like what?" she asks.

"We need to keep an eye on Greg."

"You mean follow him."

"Yes. He might get sloppy and reveal something. Or, who knows? He might even take us to the place he buried her."

"Why would he do that?"

"I don't know. People do strange things when they're feeling guilty."

Charlie sighs. "Okay. Tomorrow, Dad has a seminar for police officers or something like that. He'll be home after it's over, sometime in the afternoon. Let's give it till then to find more evidence. If we don't find anything, I think we have to take a chance, for Amy's sake, and tell my dad. Agreed?"

"Agreed," I tell her.

She nods. "So that's your plan? Follow Greg and hope he leads us to something?"

I look across the street at Greg's house, then at other houses in the neighborhood. Everything is quiet, but people will be coming home from work soon, ready to begin the weekend. TGIF and all that.

How soon before Greg's family comes home?

How easy would it be to break into his house?

"Alden…" Charlie begins.

"His backpack," I say suddenly.

"What?"

"We need to find his backpack. It's got Amy's blood on it."

"Oh, come on." She shakes her head. "I'm sure he's gotten rid of it by now."

"Maybe. Maybe not."

"He could have left it anywhere. Thrown it into a river.

Tossed it in a dumpster somewhere. If he's smart he's burned it, destroyed it."

"You said it yourself, he's no criminal mastermind."

She rolls her eyes. "Yeah, but he's not an idiot."

We do this all the time, this back-and-forth. "The only way we'll know is if we look."

"And where do we start looking?"

"Right there." I point at his house.

"What?" She looks at me like I've lost my mind. "You mean break in? Right now?"

"Not now. His parents could be home any minute."

"How are we going to do it?"

"We'll figure it out." A plan is already formulating in my head.

NINE

The baseball team practices just about every day after school, but with the team fighting for a playoff spot, weekends were added as well. Which means we know where Greg Matthes will be this Saturday morning.

It's 9:00 a.m., and baseball practice has just started. When he walked out of his house a half hour ago, I followed to make sure he went straight to practice while Charlie stayed behind to keep watch on any comings or goings.

My uncle is earning time and a half working all day Saturday, so he left before I did. Charlie's dad had already left for his workshop, and she told her mom she was leaving early to go to the gym, then she'd be spending the day with me. Maybe we'd hit the mall or see a movie. If, later, she asked what movie we saw, Charlie would name one we'd already gone to and just tell her we'd wanted to see it again.

I'm sitting on a hill that overlooks the school baseball field, watching the practice and hoping for a call from Charlie to tell me Greg's parents and sister decided to go somewhere, leaving the house empty. Then I'll head back, and we can figure out how to get in. If they don't leave before Greg is finished with practice, I'll continue to keep an eye on him and we'll have to figure something else out.

I'm not so far away that I can't see the players being put through their motions, though I'm far enough away they can't tell who I am, other than some kid with nothing better to do on a Saturday morning. My binoculars are next to me in my backpack, but using them, even at this distance, would look suspicious. Or at least weird.

Even with the distance, I recognize Greg and can tell he's off his game. I haven't been to too many school events, but I have been to a couple of baseball games. He's one of the team's best players, known for his sometimes dazzling play at third base, scooping up tough grounders and firing strong, accurate throws to first base. He also owns the second-best batting average on the team, and a reputation for good sportsmanship. He's the ideal athlete and teammate. Like I've said before: perfect.

But he's sure not perfect today. The team starts with batting practice, and all Greg is able to muster are some weak grounders and a few easy fly balls. He even whiffs several times, even though the assistant coach isn't throwing the ball that hard. After he's finished batting, the coach pulls Greg to the side to talk to him.

He probably wants to make sure his star third baseman isn't sick, with the playoffs coming up. I make note of Greg's behavior in my notebook.

After their conversation ends, the coach pats Greg on the shoulder and sends him out to field grounders at third.

He's not much better there. He starts by missing three easy ground balls in a row. Easy for him, that is; I doubt I'd be able to catch even one. When he finally fields one, he bounces the throw in the dirt well in front of the first baseman. His next is way wide, ending up far down the right-field line.

Greg definitely looks like he has something on his mind.

Something like murder.

He does better for a couple of plays, then the bad throws start up again. After one the first baseman would have to be eight feet tall to catch, the coach replaces him. He sits on the bench with his head down.

Noted.

My phone buzzes.

"We're in luck. They just left," Charlie says.

"His parents and sister?"

"No, the Scarecrow and the Tin Man. Of course, his parents and sister. And judging from what they've taken with them, they're going to be gone for a while. Looks like a picnic or something. How's practice?"

"Greg's doing terrible."

"Product of a guilty conscience."

I glance at my phone. It's 9:32. Baseball practice usually goes two and a half hours, so we should have plenty of time. "I'll be right over," I say.

Normally, it would take only ten minutes to walk to the Matthes house. I'm there in five.

I'd left Charlie on the same bench we sat last night, reading a book while keeping an eye on the Matthes house across the street. But she's not here when I jog up. Looking around, I see no sign of her. Kids are playing on the jungle gym at the far edge of the playground while parents chat, but otherwise, the playground is surprisingly empty for a Saturday morning. Where did she go?

My phone buzzes. The text from Charlie reads: *Cross the street. I'm in the backyard. Fence door is unlatched.*

I cross the street as nonchalantly as possible. I'm starting to think this is a bad idea. I feel eyes on me, like there are people watching from their windows who might find it strange I was walking into the Matthes family's backyard, but I'm in too deep to back out now.

The door to the wooden fence is unlatched, as Charlie said it would be. Checking one more time for any sign of someone watching me or dialing 911, I open the door. Charlie stands in the backyard with hands on hips, looking up. I follow her gaze to an open window on the second floor. "I checked all the other doors and windows," she says. "This is the only one open. So that's how we're getting in."

"How are we going to get up there?" I ask.

She points. "We'll use that ladder."

The ladder is leaning on its side against a shed in the far corner of the yard. "Did you break into their shed to get it?"

"Nah. It was already like that."

"Was the fence door unlocked?"

"It's just a latch."

I've had a lot of practice sneaking around. Charlie hasn't. "Did you make sure no one saw you?"

She glances over her shoulder. "We're fine." Then she looks at me. "You're not having second thoughts, are you?"

Before I can answer, Charlie continues. "Because listen, you're right. More evidence wouldn't hurt. Greg probably doesn't even have the backpack anymore. But we've got to be sure."

She eyes the ladder, then the window. "We should have plenty of time, but we can't be a hundred percent sure his family won't suddenly show up. So you stay outside and keep watch while I go in and search."

Who is this girl, and what did she do with Charlie? "Why should you go in?"

The look she gives me is almost funny. "You know I'm better suited for this." She emphasizes her point by flexing a muscle.

"But I'm the one who knows what the backpack looks like."

"I've seen Greg with the backpack at school many times. I know what it looks like. Besides," she adds, giving me a wink and a nudge, "how many backpacks can he have with blood on them?"

I can't believe how excited she is. Yesterday, I had to convince her. Now she's already cased the house and can't wait to break in.

"Hey, don't worry, it's going to go fine." She smiles. "You big goof."

"You're bigger than I am," I respond.

"Bigger and stronger. But not goofier."

I can't help but smile, too.

"If we're doing this, we should get started," Charlie says.

A good investigator understands that sometimes boundaries have to be pushed to get to the truth.

"Okay." We grab the ladder, hoist it up, and lean it against the house.

Charlie sees me pull out my cell and says, "No talking on the phone while I'm in there. I'll need to concentrate."

"All right," I agree. "But if I see them coming back, I'll text 'get out.' Then, no matter what, you get out."

"Got it. But we're fine. Plenty of time." She pats me on the shoulder and steps on the first rung of the ladder. Then she stops and steps off. "You're not staying here in the backyard, right? You have to be able to see the front door."

"Right," I say. In my head, I'm thinking, *Duh*.

"After I'm in, go out front," Charlie directs. "Watch from the playground. You'll be able to see the house and all of the street. I'll text you if I've found the backpack or when I'm finished, and you meet me at the ladder. Once I'm down, we'll put it back against the shed and get out of here, no harm, no foul. No one will know we were here."

She pats me on the shoulder again as I hold the ladder for her and starts to climb. She moves quickly. Not only is Charlie strong, she's fast. If she wanted to, she could probably be on the track team. Proving the point, she reaches the window in no time and pushes up the window to give her more room. Then, just like that, she slips inside. A few seconds later she reappears. "We're in luck. This *is* Greg's room," she calls down to me.

"Not so loud," I call back in a half whisper.

"I'm going to make a quick check through the house."

"Why?"

"I'm just being thorough. I won't be long. If I don't find it, I'll be back to search his room. You need to get out front." She commands me with a sweep of her arm. "Go."

She disappears from the window, and I hurry to the fence and open it while taking a deep breath. Then I stroll around to the front of the house, where, like before, I cross the street nonchalantly. Nothing to see here. I end up at the same bench where I'd left Charlie earlier this morning.

Some of the house's front windows have curtains, a few closed, others open, partially or completely. Hopefully Charlie is smart enough to stay where she can't be seen.

The playground has filled up. A lot more kids now run and chase each other, screaming and laughing. They throw balls and swing on swings and climb on the jungle gym while their parents chat and keep an eye on them.

Time slows to a crawl as I wait for Charlie's text telling me she's found the backpack. Not being able to see her, wondering how the search is going, makes me more nervous than I already am.

I check my phone, surprised to see only five minutes have passed since she went inside. It feels longer.

Did I just see the curtains rustling in the front window? Without thinking, I reach into my backpack for the binoculars. Before I can whip them out, a figure pops up next to me, startling me so much I practically jump out of my shoes. But it's just a boy trying to get a ball that has rolled under the bench. I reach down to pick it up and hand it to him. The boy doesn't move; he just stares at me. I'm about to ask what he wants when he grabs the ball, turns, and calls out, "I've got it!" Then he hurries off.

Strange little dude.

I glance at my phone again. Only two more minutes have gone by.

What was up with that kid? Do I look odd sitting here?

Suspicious? The way I keep shaking my leg and checking my phone every few minutes, of course I look suspicious.

Take a breath, Alden. Act casual.

I need something to do. I pull out a pen and my notebook from my backpack. Taking a moment to formulate my thoughts, I begin taking notes.

Evidence so far:

Witnessed Greg arguing with Amy.

Witnessed Amy lying on the ground, dead or unconscious.

Witnessed Greg standing over her with blood on his backpack.

Amy's body wasn't there when the police arrived. Greg must have moved it.

Amy is supposed to be at church camp. But found Amy's cross, which she is never without, lying at the spot where she was struck.

Seeing it all written down like this causes a sharp, icy chill to course through me. Time is ticking. Could Amy's life hang in the balance?

I check the time again. Charlie has now been in the house for over ten minutes. How much longer does she need? The longer this takes, the more chances a neighbor might notice something funny. Like a ladder leaning against an open upstairs window in the back of the house.

"Are you all right?" I hear behind me. I turn, expecting a cop wondering what I'm doing here, acting so nervous and writing notes. But what I heard was a father, about ten feet away, helping his teary-eyed son to his feet, brushing off grass and dirt. "You're all right," he says to the boy, giving him a hug before sending him off to play some more. Turning, he sees me looking at him and smiles. "It's okay, he's fine."

I smile back. Then I turn around and let out another long breath. Of course I check my phone again. Time seems to have sped up now. It's been almost fifteen minutes. How much longer does she need? I hope she's back in Greg's room by now.

A horrible thought comes to me: What if Charlie had an accident in there? Fell and broke her leg? Lost her phone in the fall and can't reach it, or worse, she's knocked unconscious? If she's unable to text me, how would I know anything was wrong?

A good investigator always has a plan B in case something goes wrong.

So what is my plan B? I'd have to go in and rescue her. But how long should I wait until I do something? Five more minutes? Ten? I'd have to use the ladder to get inside. But if she's hurt or unconscious, how do I get her down?

I'm getting ahead of myself. *Calm down.* I'll give her a few more minutes. If I haven't heard from her by then, I'll text and ask how much longer she thinks she'll need.

I put away my notebook and start to do the same with my pen when a sudden noise startles me, and I drop it. I pick it up as I look up and down the street. Was that a police siren? Did a neighbor see something and call the police? I hear it again. Another short, quick burst. Then a car appears, slowing down and pulling over across the street. Followed by a police car, lights flashing. It stops behind the first car.

Right in front of the Matthes house.

Stay calm, I tell myself, resisting the urge to run. For about a minute there's no movement, except for the cop talking into her handset inside her cruiser. I look over at the other car and recognize the teenager behind the wheel as a Milton High School senior, Tommy Zimmerman. And then it dawns on me. The police officer isn't here to check a report of a break-in. She pulled Tommy over, for speeding or whatever. She's probably checking his license plate with the dispatcher at the station. If I get a text from Charlie that she's ready to come out, I'll just tell her to wait.

The cop is still in her car. Tommy keeps glancing back over his shoulder at the police car and fuming, clearly unhappy. The cop finally gets out, ticket book in hand. She takes her sweet time walking to the driver's side, while Tommy rolls down his window and puts on his best innocent look.

The officer, looking very stern, begins talking. Tommy works to keep the innocent look on his face, though I can see it starting to slip. After what seems like forever, he fishes his driver's license out of his wallet and opens the glove compartment to get the car registration, handing both to the officer. The two talk some more.

What do they have to talk about? Give him the ticket and let him go on his way, jeez.

Some of the people in the playground have stopped what they were doing to watch the show playing out in front of them. I check my phone. No message. Charlie must be almost finished by now.

The cop takes Tommy's license and registration and sits in the cruiser again, writing the ticket.

I stare at her, willing her to write faster. Maybe a minute later, the officer gets out, and gives the ticket to Tommy. Then she talks to him—*Oh, for crying out loud, finish up already!*—probably giving him a lecture. Tommy's head moves like a bobblehead in agreement.

Finally, the police officer returns to her car and gets in. Tommy drives away slowly. I realize I've been holding my breath and let the air out in one long whoosh. I lean back against the bench, watching the police cruiser pull away from the curb.

And there's Greg Matthes walking down the street, just one house away from his own home.

What the hell is he doing here already? Practice shouldn't be over by now. Whatever. It doesn't matter. All that matters is he's here. Now.

And Charlie's still inside.

My fingers feel like fat sausages as I text *GET OUT*.

He approaches his front door. I want to disappear into the bench, but he doesn't seem to notice me. Greg fishes for his keys while my foot taps frantically on the ground. He inserts a key into the doorknob, then goes inside, shutting the door.

I bolt across the street, not caring about being nonchalant. Pushing through the fence door, I hurry to where the ladder is still leaning against the house. I look up at the window of Greg's room. *Come on, Charlie, where are you?*

And then I see her. She has nothing with her; I guess she didn't find the backpack. She sees me, waves, then begins to step out of the window and onto the highest step of the ladder. I hold it steady for her.

But with one foot out, she stops and puts her hand up. Then she hisses "*Hide!*" and abruptly disappears *back* into the room. I call out her name in my own harsh whisper, but she doesn't respond. I run to the shed, my backpack in hand, before looking back. I don't see Charlie. Then Greg enters his room. He turns toward the open window, and I duck behind the shed.

I take a moment to control my runaway heartbeat before I peer out from my hiding place. It doesn't seem like Greg saw me, but has he found Charlie? Is she hiding? He's standing near the window, doing nothing for the moment. If he glances down, he'll see the ladder leaning against the house. Thankfully, he moves away, out of sight.

I reach into my backpack, pulling out my notebook first, then the binoculars. I creep out from behind the shed; I can always duck back if I have to. Using the binoculars, I focus in on Greg talking to someone on his phone. He doesn't seem angry like he did the last time I saw him like this, though it does look like *something's* bothering him.

I can see most of the room now. It's big. There are posters of sports stars I don't recognize on a brown-paneled wall, a bed, and a worn recliner pushed against one corner. A shelf next to his bed is full of gaudy trophies, and more cover the entire top of an end table on the other side. There's a closet, and a desk with a laptop on it. His room is nice. And clean, of course. Much nicer and cleaner than mine.

Where is Charlie?

The call seems go on forever. Greg paces from one side of the room to the other, before he finally finishes and tosses his phone on his bed. He slips off his practice shirt and, shirtless, he crosses to the closet. My stomach tightens as he opens the door. Could Charlie have gone in there? But all he does is pull a button-down shirt from a hangar and put it on. Through the binoculars, I try peering inside the closet, but I can't see much.

Leaving the closet door open, he walks to the center of the room. He seems to be thinking again. I had no idea he was such a big thinker. He needs to get out so Charlie can escape. What if he decides to take a nap or read a book or who knows what?

A plan begins to formulate as I watch Greg head back to the

closet. This time he pushes aside hanging clothes, walking in deeper until I can't see him. If Charlie is hiding in there, he's sure to find her now. I wait, tense, expecting to see Greg yanking Charlie out of the closet any second. What do I do if that happens? I keep the binoculars trained on the closet, my fingers hurting from holding them so tight.

My muscles relax as he reappears without Charlie. If I'm going to do something to get him out of his room, I need to do it now. I stand up and take a deep breath. My legs won't move. *Do it! Now!*

I run across the backyard, reach the fence, and push open the door, racing toward the front porch. There are fewer people at the playground, and thankfully, none of them are looking my way.

My plan in place, I ring the doorbell.

When Greg doesn't come to the door, I ring again and peer through the front window. There's movement on a second-floor landing, then feet on the stairs.

I hurry back around the house. Charlie is at the window. She waves at me, but instead of climbing out of the window, she gives me a wait-a-minute sign and turns from view. I wait nervously, hopping from one leg to the other. Greg has definitely seen no one was at the front door by now. *Hurry up, hurry up!*

Again, I run around to the front of the house, where I ring the bell twice, then hurry back to the rear of the house, praying for the best.

Framed in the window, Charlie gives me a big smile as she lifts up what she's holding in her hand. It takes me a moment to realize what it is.

Greg's backpack.

Greg's *bloody* backpack.

Oh God, she's touching it. Why didn't we think of this? It's going to get contaminated with her DNA. Too late to do anything about it now. I motion for her to hurry. First, she throws out the backpack, and it lands at my feet. Then she's out of the window and climbing down the ladder so fast she's a third of the way down by the time I'm steadying it. Without warning, she jumps, bringing the ladder with her. I manage to grab it before it hits me, then together we lean it haphazardly against the shed. Charlie hoists the backpack onto her shoulder and says, "Let's go."

My backpack! As Charlie runs toward the fence door, I head behind the shed, where I grab it and my binoculars. There's no sign of Greg at the windows, and Charlie is waiting for me with the fence door open, so I take off toward her, and, together, we burst out of the backyard. Keeping up with Charlie isn't easy, but I run like I've never run before, praying that Greg isn't watching.

TEN

The Matthes house is the only one for several blocks with a fence, so we stick to backyards until we feel safe enough to return to the front sidewalk and slow our pace.

Charlie's house is closer, so we end up there. Once inside, we collapse on the couch; Charlie drops the infamous backpack at our feet. We may have slowed to a walk for the last few blocks, but my heart is still pounding against my chest. "Are you sure your mom's not coming home soon?" I ask.

Charlie laughs. "I told you, she's shopping and having lunch with a friend today. She won't be home until midafternoon." She takes a deep breath, then blurts out, "That was exciting," before bursting into fresh laughter. After another moment, she asks, "Do you want some ginger ale?"

She knows that's my favorite soda. "Sure." By the time she's back with two cans of ginger ale, she's laughing again. Handing me one, she pops the other, and after drinking half of the can, she declares, "If I had known being a criminal was so much fun, I might have tried it a long time ago."

"I was scared," I tell her.

"Scared? You big goof." She's about to laugh again, but when I don't come back with the usual response, she stops and puts her soda on the coffee table. "All right, yeah, it was scary. But that's part of what makes it fun. And look!" She lifts Greg's backpack in triumph. "We got it!"

When I don't respond, she drops the bag back on the floor, then sits back, frowning at me.

Finally, I break the silence. "He almost caught us."

"Did you see the phone conversation he was having?" Charlie says. "He was talking to a friend. Told him the coach sent him home because he was playing so poorly. He blamed himself, not the coach. Even after killing somebody, he comes off like Mr. Goody Two-Shoes."

"I figured that's what it was."

"Yeah, well, everything's good now."

"We just threw the ladder back. What if they notice?" I say.

"They won't."

"You can't know that."

"It was close enough," she says. "He won't notice."

"He might once he realizes his backpack is gone. He'll know someone is on to him."

"Will you chill out? Even if he does realize his backpack is gone, he won't know we took it," she says.

"He will once we give the backpack to your dad."

Now Charlie scowls at me. "This was your idea, you know." She sits back and takes another sip. "Greg won't have to know it came from us," she says. "At least not right away. Not until you have to testify about what you saw."

My stomach turns inside out. I hadn't considered the possibility I might have to testify in court. In front of all those people. In front of Greg Matthes.

"You know, he might not find out the backpack's gone," Charlie says. "Not for a while, anyway."

"How do you figure?"

"He didn't just have it hidden in the closet. He'd put it under some loose floorboards. I'd already checked the closet. I wouldn't even have known I'd missed it if he hadn't gotten it out himself. When you rang the doorbell the first time, he put it back. I went into the closet, saw one of the floorboards sort of sticking out, pulled it up, and found the backpack. If he doesn't check for it..." She shrugs.

"Where were you hiding?" I ask. "I couldn't tell."

"Behind a chest of drawers in the corner of the room right next to the window."

"That was dangerous," I say.

"Best I could do. And if I'd gotten out before he came in, I wouldn't have seen him get the backpack out, so we're all good. We got away, and Greg didn't see us."

Charlie picks up the backpack. I remember my concern about DNA, but I guess it doesn't matter if she keeps touching it. "I can't figure out why he's holding on to this, though," she says. "He should have thrown it away as far from here as he could. Or maybe it's got sentimental value, and he hopes he can clean the blood off. That'd be pretty stupid on his part."

She takes a closer look at the blood showing on the front pocket. "There's not as much blood as I thought there'd be, the way you talked about it."

She's right. At the time, I'd thought blood covered the entire front, not just the pocket. Most of the blood I see now could probably be covered with both of my hands.

"But nobody ever said there has to be a lot of blood to kill somebody," Charlie says. She shakes the bag. "Before you rang the doorbell, I thought he was about to reach inside it for something, but it feels empty." She zips it open, reaches in, and moves her hand around. Then she checks the pockets, unzipping each one. Finally, she shrugs. "Like I said, empty." The bag ends up on the couch between us.

"So I guess we take it to my father after his workshop," Charlie says.

A good investigator collects all the evidence he needs before making an accusation.

"It's not enough," I hear myself say.

"What do you mean not enough?" Charlie is getting that look she gets.

"You weren't sure you believed me when I told you what I saw."

"Until we found her cross," Charlie reminds me.

"Your father will come up with a lot of reasons for why that cross was there, all of which don't end with her being dead."

"The bloody backpack—"

"He'll say we don't know where the blood came from."

"But you'll say you saw the blood right after Greg struck Amy with it."

"It's not enough," I say again. "We need more."

"It's enough to make him call her parents. Then call the camp, wherever it is, and find out she's not there."

"Your dad will still say it doesn't mean she's dead."

"So what? He'll still investigate. Isn't that what you want?"

"I was sure that the man in the mall had a gun," I say. "And I was sure Gavin was carrying a gun at school. And look what happened. I need to be absolutely sure."

"Well, I'm sure," Charlie says. "You've convinced me. Unless you're changing your story."

"I'm not."

"Because if after making me believe you and getting me to help you—"

I cut her off, my voice rising. "What's wrong with wanting to get more evidence before telling your dad?"

"Well, Alden, what'd you have in mind?" Her voice is louder than mine now. "Shall we go to Greg and ask him, 'Did you kill Amy? 'Cause if you did, it sure would be helpful to us if you'd go tell my father, just so, you know, we have enough *evidence*—'"

The sudden sound of the front door opening catches us both by surprise. Hearing the familiar heavy footsteps, my eyes go directly to the bloody backpack still on the couch, my legs unable to move. But Charlie reacts quickly, grabbing the backpack and dropping it behind the couch just as her father strides into the room. A bear of a man, he makes an impressive figure wearing his police chief uniform. Or, sometimes, a scary one, like he does now. He's staring at us, maybe because he thinks something is up—probably because we look guilty. Probably using the same gaze he uses to get a confession out of a suspect when he needs one.

It seems to take forever, though it's probably just a second or two, before he says, "Are you two doing something I should know about?" he says.

Crap, he knows! How could he know?

To her credit, Charlie doesn't flinch as she puts a smile on her face and crosses the room. "Hi, Dad." She plants a kiss on his cheek. "Catch any bad guys today?"

He studies her face before responding. "Yep," he says. He sounds wary. Being a cop for as long as he has, he's probably naturally suspicious. "The streets of Milton are safe for another day." A big grin now takes over his face. Charlie and I both laugh; hers sounds natural while mine sounds tight and forced. The bloody backpack is blocked, for the moment, by the couch, but all Charlie's dad has to do is move a couple of feet to his right to see it.

"Actually, I've been involved in that seminar," Chief Walker says. "But weren't you two going to a movie today?"

"It's not even noon yet," his daughter says. "Too early. We're just hanging out until then." Charlie's smile seems normal. I'm sure mine looks as forced as my laugh.

"Thought you were working all day," Charlie says. "Are you finished early?"

"I wish. This seminar crap is torture." Giving his daughter a wink, he adds, "Pretend you didn't hear that."

Charlie winks back. I react with what is supposed to be a laugh but quickly turns into a nervous cough.

Father and daughter both look at me. Then Chief Walker says, "I've got to get back. We're on a break. I forgot something I need and came home to get it. I'm not sure where I left it, though." He starts looking around the room. My legs don't move, but Charlie slides to the side, blocking his view of the backpack with her body. "Maybe we can help. What are you looking for?"

"Hmm, now that I think about it, it's probably upstairs in my study." He heads for the stairs, and I breathe a sigh of relief. Looking over his shoulder, he adds, "Charlie, would you make me a bologna sandwich? I don't think I'm going to be able to come home for lunch. Just a little mayo, remember."

"Okay, Dad," she says, heading toward the kitchen.

Still frozen in place, I watch Charlie's dad march up the stairs.

"Alden," comes softly from the kitchen, but I'm too focused on the stairs to respond.

"Alden!" Charlie tries again, her voice raised to a harsh whisper this time. I turn toward her.

"Quick, hide it," she says.

"Hide…"

"Before he gets back. *Hurry!*"

Charlie bangs around in the kitchen while I look frantically around the room. There's the coffee table, another chair, a fireplace, and a couple of side tables, none of which work as a hiding place. A closet door for coats and such sits partially open. My legs finally moving, I pick up the backpack, and when I hear heavy footsteps moving toward the stairs, I quickly fling it into the closet.

Oh crap. Now I've touched it, too.

"Not there!" Charlie whispers loudly from the kitchen. "He might—"

Too late. Chief Walker is starting down the stairs. If I tried to close the closet door, it would look suspicious. Instead, I sit on the couch, trying not to look guilty, as he comes into view.

"Found it!" Chief Walker announces, waving something in the air, then sticking it inside his jacket so quickly I can't tell what is. "Got that sandwich ready for me, honey?"

Charlie walks out of the kitchen with a lunch bag. "I threw in honey barbecue chips, a chocolate cupcake, and an apple."

"Always looking out for me, aren't you?" he says, taking the bag and kissing her on the cheek. "Wish I could eat lunch with you here. Though at least this way you two can continue with whatever top-secret stuff you were planning when I walked in." This last he says with a mischievous grin on his face, which he directs first toward his daughter, then toward me. I try to smile back, but I can't seem to get my mouth to work.

"Yeah, that's right, Dad." Charlie arches an eyebrow. "The second you walk out that door, we're going to do some serious making out."

Chief Walker shakes his head at his daughter. "Good thing I know you're kidding. Good thing I know I can *trust* you, right, Alden?" I've seen this back-and-forth between father and daughter before, and I never know how to react. Especially now that he's looking at me again, smiling at me with what feels like a touch of warning. Not that Charlie and I have ever thought of messing around; still, to him, I'm sure the smile I manage this time makes me look like it's all I think about.

"Dad, stop teasing Alden."

"He knows I'm kidding." After the smallest of pauses, he says, "Right, Alden?"

"Don't answer," Charlie says. "You'll just encourage him."

"All right, all right. I should probably go," he says. "What movie are you two seeing?"

I start to say the first title that pops into my head, but Charlie quickly cuts me off. "We don't know yet."

"Pick a comedy. You both look like you could use a laugh." Lunch bag in hand, he starts toward the front door. And stops.

He turns toward the closet. Oh, crap. I should say something to make him stop, but my mind is as frozen as my legs were earlier. I glance at Charlie; she looks as helpless as I feel.

He's going to see the backpack. Our investigation is about to be uncovered.

He reaches the closet. Touches the door.

The sound of the door clicking shut makes me jump.

"No need for that to be sitting open," he mumbles. Then he looks at us. "Enjoy the movie." With that, he's gone, the front door closing behind him like a gunshot.

Charlie runs to the window and parts the curtains to peek out. "That was close," she says. A few seconds later, she pulls them closed. "Okay, he's left."

She opens the closet door and yanks out the backpack.

"Do you think he saw it?" I ask.

"Of course not. He'd have said something if he did." Despite all her bluster, her legs seem to wobble a little as she plops down next to me and hands over the backpack. "If you're so set on finding more evidence before we give it to him, we can't keep this here."

It sits heavily on my lap, even though it's empty. "What about your deadline for telling your dad?" I ask.

She gives me that hard stare of hers, but quickly drops it. "You still think we need more evidence?"

"Yes."

"I guess…"

"What!"

She looks at me. "Seeing the blood on the backpack makes me… You think Amy's dead, don't you?"

I hesitate only briefly. "Yes."

"Then I guess…if Amy's dead, what's a couple more days? She'll still be dead."

Something cold and slithery crawls up my spine. "That's harsh."

Charlie shrugs. "Yeah. But it's true."

She's right. Waiting an extra day or two to report the crime isn't going to hurt Amy. And using the extra time to look for more evidence might solve her murder.

"How are you planning to find more evidence?" Charlie asks.

"By keeping an eye on Greg," I answer.

"By following him, you mean."

"It's the only thing I can think of right now. Maybe he'll do something that will give himself away."

"You want to go back to his house today?"

"No. Me ringing his doorbell might have his radar up now. I'll do it tomorrow."

"You need some help?"

I think a minute. "I don't know. I might do better on my own. I'll let you know."

She seems taken aback. "You have until Monday," she says after a few seconds. "Then whether we have more or not, we tell my dad."

"Okay," I say. I lift the backpack. "In the meantime, I'll hide this at my place. Uncle Bill will never see it."

"If we're not doing anymore today, I say we pick out a movie and go to it. Better that than come up with a reason why we didn't go."

Like Charlie's dad suggested, we pick out a comedy. But first we stop by my house, where, after dropping off my backpack, I put Greg's backpack in a bag along with the necklace and hide it in the farthest corner of my closet. Uncle Bill never comes into my room, so I know it's safe.

ELEVEN

When I get home, my uncle's already asleep in his armchair in front of the TV, a half-eaten sandwich next to him on a small table. He's tired all the time, and I know it's because he thinks he needs to support me the way my parents did, so he works these long hours. I wish he could understand I don't need *things*—I'm just happy to have *him*, even if I don't respond well when he brings up my parents. I head upstairs, where I sit down at my desk to make notes in my notebook.

A good investigator always keeps thorough notes of the case he's on.

My notebook! I can't find it! I dig frantically through my backpack. Everything else is there. But not my notes. My heart pounds as I go around the room looking for it, in drawers, under my bed, everywhere. Nothing! Everything I've written since my parents were killed, all the work I've done—gone! My pulse races as I try to think back: When did I last have it? I remember writing in it while sitting on the bench across the street from the Matthes house, waiting for Charlie to finish her search. But I distinctly remember putting it back in my bag before I ran over there. Did I pull it out again at some point to make more notes? I don't think so, not with all the craziness going on. The last thing I remember pulling out of my bag was the binoculars I used to see Greg in his room.

Wait. When I pulled the binoculars out earlier, I pulled the notebook out first because it was in the way. Which means I left it behind the shed. Where anybody in the Matthes family—including Greg—could find it!

I have to go back. Tonight.

As desperate as I am to get going, I wait until I hear Uncle Bill stirring below, worried that I'll hyperventilate and pass out before he gets upstairs. I'm on my bed, not even seeing the words in the book I hold open in front of me as he stops at my door. "What'd you do today?" he asks, rubbing his eyes.

"Hung out with Charlie. Saw a movie."

"Was it good?"

"It was okay."

"Did you get dinner?"

"I ate at Charlie's."

He nods. "Good." He scratches his face. "I'm not working a double shift tomorrow, so I'll be home in time for dinner. We could order pizza from that place you like."

"Uh…sure." *Will you go to bed already?*

"You got plans tomorrow?" he asks.

"Just homework. I'll probably go to the library. And see what Charlie is doing." *And, oh yeah, I'm going to be following a murderer around.*

"That Charlie, she's a nice girl. Are the two of you…you know…"

"We're just friends," I say. *Come on, come on!*

He nods his head, looking a little embarrassed for asking. "Your dad had his share of girlfriends in high school. He was always better at talking to girls than I was. Of course, once he met your mom…" His voice trails off.

Does he really have to talk about this now? My chest feels like it's going to burst.

"You okay?" he asks.

"What? I'm fine. Just…a little tired." I fake an elaborate yawn.

He stares a moment before finally saying, "Okay then. Good night."

"Good night," I say, thinking I might have hurt his feelings as he shuffles down the hall to his bedroom. But I can't do anything about it now.

I want to go rushing out of the house, but I force myself to wait until I hear his familiar snoring, then wait an additional fifteen minutes to be sure before grabbing my backpack and creeping out of the house as fast as I can.

TWELVE

Charlie let me hold on to her extra bike, so I use it to pedal madly to the playground across from the Matthes house. The sky is cloudy with only a quarter moon, which should make it easier to sneak around the backyard. I crouch down near a bush and stare at the house, looking for any sign of movement. It's after ten, but it's Saturday, so some of the Matthes clan might be out, Greg included. Or is Milton High's perfect student always in by ten, regardless of the day?

A few lights are on downstairs. I see only a single upstairs light on.

I wait a while, not sure how much time has passed since I got here. Every now and then I think I see shadows beyond the curtains, indicating movement. Looks like someone is in there. More time passes. What am I waiting for? Some kind of assurance? How do I get that? By hoping the entire family is going to come out of the house and drive away together? That's not going to happen. And the garage door is closed, so I can't tell if one or both of the family cars are inside. I'll just have to be careful and hope no one sees me. If I'm going to do this, it needs to be now.

The thought crosses my mind that somebody may have found the notebook already, maybe Greg. He may have even read it. The idea causes a sharp pain to cut through my chest, and makes me want to grab the bike and pedal my way out of here.

But I don't. I have to know. Slowly, I straighten up, take in a couple of deep breaths, then a couple more. It's now or never. Too bad my legs don't seem to want to move. Then, suddenly, I'm off and running across the street, onto the Matthes property, across the front yard. I stop at the fence and slowly lift the latch. The click it makes seems as loud as a gunshot. I freeze, convinced everyone in the neighborhood heard it. I wait a few seconds. Nothing. Just the sound of crickets and a TV playing a little too loud from another house in the neighborhood. Now that I'm close, I realize I don't hear anything from inside. No TV or radio. Maybe no one is home. I slide into the backyard. The ladder still leans against the shed where we left it. The thin moon offers little light, but I don't even think about turning on the flashlight on my phone.

Another deep breath and I'm running again, dodging behind the shed. I drop to my knees, running my hands through the grass. It has to be here. Unless someone did find it. I remember squatting right here. Taking a chance, I turn on my phone's flash-light hoping the shed will block the sudden brightness. Light bounces over the ground.

There! It's in the grass, a good five feet or more from where I'd envisioned it. Did I really toss it that far in my hurry to get the binoculars? It doesn't feel right. As I pick up my notebook, another possibility comes to mind, sending a chill through me: that Greg found it and left it here to see who came back for it.

Moving slowly, I peer out. Any lights on are in the front, so it's hard to see through the windows. My eyes drift up to Greg's window. The curtains had been open this morning, but now they're closed. The lights in the room are off, but is that movement? Like someone is parting the curtains just enough to see out? I duck back behind the shed. The feeling that someone is spying on me doesn't go away.

As I try peering out again, a flash of light appears on the far right, on the other side of the fence. Two lights. Headlights. A car turning into the Mattheses' driveway. The garage door groans as it opens.

Fortunately, the fence door is on the opposite side of the house from the garage. Throwing my notebook in my bag, I hurry across the grass. The latch pops again as I open it, but the slam of car doors and the sound of people talking mute it. Instead of running across the street, I hide behind a bush in the neighbor's front yard. Greg's parents, who I recognize from church, step out of the garage. The front door of the house opens, and Greg and his little sister appear. She runs to her parents and hugs them while Greg glances up and down the street, and I instinctively shrink back. When his parents get to the door, his father asks, "Did you two stay out of trouble?"

"I won every game of Chutes and Ladders," his sister says.

"Are you sure your brother didn't let you win?" her father says, grinning at Greg.

"I beat him fair and square."

"Uh, yeah, you did," Greg tells his sister with a tentative smile.

Greg had been babysitting his sister. Playing games with her. So maybe he wasn't looking out of his window to see me retrieving my notebook.

I breathe a little easier.

But as soon as they enter the house, his smile vanishes, and he glances up and down the street once more before closing the door.

Moving away, I cross the street farther down, then hurry back to the playground. With more resolve than ever to find the evidence I need, I jump on Charlie's bike and pedal furiously toward home.

THIRTEEN

The last shot was fired, followed by silence.
Fired by the shooter, having saved the last bullet for himself, it
turned out. As I learned later, the police who'd been there to offer
security for the fair had not gotten off a single shot while the shooter
had gotten off eight rounds, with six of them finding their targets.
The whole thing took less than a minute.

Within seconds there were people crying, calling for help, and
police shouting out orders.

So many voices. "Get over here!"

"Here's another one. Just lay still. Help is coming."

"Christ, how many are there?"

"Four, I think. They're all alive. Is there anybody else shot?"

"I don't think so. I don't see…"

"Did someone call for ambulances?"

"I did. They're on their way."

Chaos. Confusion. A woman screamed. A male voice said, "Don't try to move—it's okay. It'll be okay."

Then two men were talking. Cops, maybe?

"Is he dead?"

"Yeah, he's dead. Blew the back of his head off."

"Good. It saved me from doing it for him."

"Do you recognize him?"

"Never saw him before in my life."

All at once, Chief Walker appeared above me. "Can you get up, Alden?" he asked. I nodded, and he helped me up, eyes running up and down my body. I realized I have blood all down the front of me. "Are you *shot*?"

"I...I don't think..."

He looked past me at the ground, his face turning ashen. "Oh, Christ," he muttered. Then turning, he shouted, "I need help over here, right now! *Right now!* Where are those goddamn ambulances?"

And as if on cue, I heard sirens far in the distance, but I was looking down at what had caused the police chief's face to drain of color.

I remembered my father trying to pull me down, protect me, but I'd somehow ended up on top of my parents; it was their blood on me. My father was now lying partially on top of my mother, his right arm around her shoulder, as if he had hoped to protect her, too. Blood from both of them continued to flow out, mingling together.

"Hurry!" Chief Walker shouted, louder, almost screaming. "*Hurry!*"

There were tears on his face before another police officer gently pulled me aside. "Over here, sweetheart," she said in a kind voice. "Let them do their work."

And, again, as if on cue, two paramedics arrived, crouching down to check on my mom and dad. Chief Walker appeared again, this time with Dr. Taubin, one of our local physicians. The doctor must have been attending the summer fair. "I don't think it's his blood," the police chief said, "but could you check him out for me, Joe?"

The doctor said, "Sure, Matt," and gave me the once-over. I couldn't remember what either of us had said. "No wounds," he told Charlie's father. "But I think he's in shock. You should have him looked at at the hospital."

Where was Charlie? I'd been talking to her just a few minutes ago. Or was it an hour ago? I wasn't sure.

I'm watching the paramedics and the doctor continue to work on my parents. I should be crying at least, or screaming, or begging the paramedics to please save my mother and father, but nothing seemed real.

At one point, I found myself walking toward the body of the shooter, who was lying on his back, uncovered, on the ground. Blood and brain matter formed a pattern on the grass at his head, but I was staring at his eyes, which were wide open, and his mouth was frozen in a half smile, as if, even in death, he was glad about what he'd done.

His name, Alan Harder, would be in the news every day for the next week, as would many theories as to why he did it—most, if not all of them, only guesses. But that day, at that moment, before the officer returned to put her arm around me and steer me toward Chief Walker's car in order to follow the ambulances carrying my parents to the hospital—before all that, I stared at the face of the man who had killed my parents.

And realized I had seen him before.

FOURTEEN

Apparently, Uncle Bill was never much of a churchgoer, but that changed when he became my guardian. He knew Dad and Mom had taken me to church most Sundays, and he was determined to continue the weekly tradition. At first. But lately, as work has piled up, making him more tired than usual, we've missed some Sunday services. Missed the last two Sundays, in fact, which has suited me just fine. Any interest I might have had in attending church has been pretty much gone since my parents' deaths.

But this particular Sunday morning is different. I want to go. That's because the Matthes family will be there. They go almost as often as Amy Sloan's family; with Mr. and Mrs. Sloan out of town, this might be the first Sunday service they've missed in years. Greg even goes on the few Sundays when the rest of his family aren't there, so he can be with Amy. He and Amy always sit together. Not this morning, though. People will think it's because Amy's at church camp, but I know the truth. So does Greg, and I want to see how it affects him.

If he shows up at all.

I'm already dressed and eating cereal when Uncle Bill trudges downstairs, scratching his crotch, still dressed in the lounge pants and worn-out T-shirt he wears to sleep in. Seeing me, he stops at the bottom of the stairs, surprised.

"You're dressed already," he says, taking note of my black slacks and light blue polo shirt.

"Yeah," I say. "Church."

"I was thinking…uh…maybe we wouldn't go this morning," Uncle Bill says. "We'd just sleep in."

"But you're up," I point out.

"I was just coming down to get the paper, some coffee, then go back to sleep for a bit before I have to go to work."

"We haven't been in a couple weeks," I remind him.

He doesn't seem to know how to answer that and fumbles for words. "Well, uh… Well, I guess…" He looks upstairs longingly, as if his bedsheets are calling to him to get back under them. "Just let me change…"

"I'll go by myself," I say.

He looks at me. "I just need a minute—"

"I'm serious. You're right. You've been really busy. You need the rest. Sleep in until you have to go to work. I'll be fine going to church by myself."

"How will you get there?" Uncle Bill asks.

"I have one of Charlie's bikes. I'll use that."

"Well, if you're sure…"

"I'm sure."

"Okay then." He hesitates, then asks, "You've got plans this afternoon?"

"Like I said last night, homework. I'll probably go to the library."

"Right." He nods. "I'll be home by seven. I'll bring pizza with me. You want the usual?"

"Sure." I keep smiling as he heads back upstairs, apparently forgetting his intention to get the newspaper and coffee, just happy to get a little more sleep, which makes me feel more guilty about all the hours he puts in so he can take care of me.

FIFTEEN

I arrive at church five minutes before the 10:00 a.m. service is scheduled to begin, with the sanctuary about three-quarters full. There's an open space at the end of a pew next to Charlie, whose parents are sitting next to her on her left. Her mom says, "Hello, Alden," and her dad nods a greeting to me, then glances around the room, looking for my uncle. It's not uncommon for me to sit next to Charlie and her family on the Sundays she and I both attend while Uncle Bill sits across the aisle by himself. He could sit with me if he wants, but he seems to prefer being alone, looking very solemn and sad, with his head down most of the time. Still mourning my parents, my father—his brother—in particular, after all these months.

When he doesn't see him anywhere, Chief Walker seems about to say something to me before changing his mind and turning his gaze back to the front of the church. I hadn't thought about how strange it might look, me coming here by myself.

Charlie leans toward me and whispers, "Where's your uncle?"

"He decided to sleep in before he has to go to work," I whisper back.

I expect her to ask why I would come alone then, but she's no dummy. I watch her gaze go to the third row where the Matthes family is sitting, where they always sit every Sunday; Greg, with no Amy here, sits between his father and little sister. After a moment, she leans toward me again and whispers, "Be careful. Don't overdo it."

After another minute of waiting, Reverend Davis stands and approaches the altar, and the service begins.

While I've taught myself how to keep an eye on someone without flat-out staring, I've never tried it in a room with this many people. Greg and his family are three rows in front of me, which is good. But they are sitting to my right. If they were on my left I could watch Greg while also looking at the minister as he talked. But in order to see Greg and still keep my gaze pointed toward the altar, I need to watch him from the corner of my eye without turning my head too much. It's not easy to do, and at one point, after catching myself staring too long at Greg, I find Chief Walker frowning at me. Keeping my calm, I act as if I didn't notice and return my attention to the pastor. I keep my gaze toward the altar for a good five minutes before going back to watching Greg in the periphery.

During announcements, when the preacher brings up the "precious young people from our congregation who have been attending camp this weekend" each by name, Greg seems to flinch when he mentions Amy. Later in the service, the pastor sermonizes about the destruction of keeping secrets from our loved ones, and I notice Greg pulling his gaze away from the minister. He puts his head down and stays that way.

I wish I had my notebook to write this all down.

At one point while focusing on Greg, I feel a sudden jab in my side, and I turn to see Charlie glaring at me with the tray of communion bread in her hand. As she passes it along, I notice her father frowning at me again. He turns, and I concentrate on chewing communion until it liquefies in my mouth.

Greg still has his head down. At one point, his father looks at him then leans over to say something. Greg nods and keeps his head up after that, watching the pastor. When Pastor Davis asks the congregation to rise, Greg is a little slow to move. His sister jabs him, and at first he seems annoyed, but once he's on his feet, he smiles at her, whispering something that makes her giggle, and prompts a frown from Mr. Matthes.

He seems normal for the remainder of the service. Just another typical Sunday morning.

Except I know it's not typical.

I notice more than Greg during the service. People look at me too. Nothing obvious, just quick, furtive glances. Maybe it's because this is the first time I've come to church by myself, but I think it's something else.

I know the look, and I understand it. People were very nice, very kind to me right after the shooting. Even classmates who had paid no attention to me before offered me words of condolence. But it's been ten months since my parents were killed, and, still, people give me looks of pity, or sadness, or try to convey how brave they think I am. Like they thought I would've just gone into hiding after what happened and never come out. I understand them, though. They want to be compassionate. And they're doing their best.

What's worse are those who look at me as if they're grateful. Grateful that what happened to me didn't happen to them. Thank God *they* didn't lose any loved ones that day. Thank God it was my parents who died that day and not *them*.

So many people in this town have known me since I was born, have watched me grow up. But I'm not that Alden Ross anymore. Now I'm Alden Ross whose parents were killed.

A living, breathing reminder of that awful day.

Once the service is over, people make their way toward the exit. I walk out with Charlie while her parents hang back to talk to friends. As always, Reverend Davis is positioned at the church's front door so he can shake hands with each congregation member as they leave the building. It's virtually impossible to avoid talking to the preacher without looking like you're snubbing him.

"So nice to see you, Alden," he says when I reach him, shaking my hand vigorously, a broad smile on his face. "I've missed you the past two Sundays. How are you doing, son?"

"I'm fine," I answer.

"I didn't see your Uncle Bill today," he notes, looking around. "In fact, I haven't seen him in a few weeks. I hope he's feeling all right."

"He's fine. He's just been busy."

"Oh, I see." He's still smiling, but judgment flashes in his eyes. "Well, you be sure to tell him I was asking about him."

"I will," I say. And, knowing Uncle Bill, once I tell him, he'll be sure to be at church next Sunday, no matter how tired he feels. I can't blame Reverend Davis for laying on a little guilt, though. He performed the funeral service for my parents, and it was clear he'd put some thought into it. He didn't just go with some canned remarks. He'd chosen a few scriptures I know Mom was fond of and had us all sing three hymns my Mom and Dad had enjoyed. And his sermon had included personal stories about them, emphasizing the humor that had been so much a part of their lives.

Of our lives.

I really appreciated that.

Walking away as other people move up to greet the minister, Charlie mutters to me, "Could you have been more obvious?"

"What?" I ask.

"You might as well have been wearing a sign saying, 'I'm here to spy on Greg Matthes.'"

"It wasn't that bad."

"It was close."

"You just noticed because you knew what I was doing. Nobody else did."

"My dad might have picked up on it a couple of times."

We come to a stop. Beyond Charlie's right shoulder, I see the Matthes family, Greg included, greeting Reverend Davis. Charlie's parents are next, patiently waiting their turn.

"Did you notice Greg flinch when the reverend mentioned Amy's name?" I ask Charlie.

"Yeah," she says. "Maybe."

The mention of Greg's name causes both of us to look at him. He's shaking the pastor's hand and smiling. Reverend Davis laughs at something Greg says. Whatever it was, I'm sure it was brilliant.

After moving out of the line, Greg gives his mom and dad each a hug. Then he picks up his sister and hugs her, too.

"Looks like he's leaving," Charlie says.

"Yeah," I agree.

"Aren't you going to follow him?"

"I know where he's going."

"So did you learn anything spying on him here? Or were you hoping to stare him into standing up and confessing to killing Amy in front of everyone?"

"That would have made things easy." I watch him walking quickly away from his parents. He's clearly not the angry, frustrated Greg I saw at practice yesterday. He's more in control, though he still looks like someone with something on his mind. Someone happy to get away from other people so he can drop the everything-is-fine act, if for just a little while.

Clearly, he hasn't gone back to the hiding place in his closet to learn that his backpack stained with Amy's blood is gone. How is he going to react when that happens? Will he be able to keep up the pretense then? And what's going to happen when Amy's parents come home Monday night and their daughter is missing?

"You sure you don't want my help today?" Charlie asks.

"I'm sure." Charlie looks disappointed, so I add, "It'll be easier and less conspicuous if only one person follows him instead of two. I'll call you if I need you. Or if something big happens."

"You'd better," she says.

"I will. I promise." I don't want to tell her the other reason I want to do this alone: that maybe she had too much fun breaking into Greg's house, pushing the limits a little further than they should be pushed.

"Okay," she says. "And call me tonight no matter what."

Before I have a chance to respond to that, Charlie's parents appear. "What are you two talking about?" her father asks.

Without missing a beat, Charlie says, "I was telling Alden I think I just saw Jesus and now I'm saved."

Chief Walker frowns at his daughter but can't help but grin. Mrs. Walker shakes her head at both of them and says, "I'd say something if I thought it'd do any good." Then she turns to me and asks, "Would you like to have lunch with us at the diner? If your uncle isn't busy, he could join us there."

"Uncle Bill's working today," I say. Thinking fast, I add, "I've got this big homework assignment I've been putting off. I've really got to work on it today."

"I've been telling you that you needed to get started on that," Charlie says, a big, fake smile on her face that's as much about her being mad that I'm not letting her go with me as it is about her backing up my story. Neither of her parents seem to notice.

"Well, if you change your mind, you know where we'll be," Chief Walker says, slapping me on the shoulder.

"See you later," Charlie says as she and her parents head toward their car. When her mom and dad aren't looking, she brings an invisible phone receiver to her ear and mouths, "Call me." I nod, and she gets in the car with her parents.

Greg is nowhere in sight now, but like I told Charlie, I know where he's going.

SIXTEEN

I stop at home to drop off the bike because it'll be easier to follow Greg on foot. I hurry to change clothes and grab snacks to take with me. I choose a different place than I did yesterday to watch the field from, this one a little farther away. I can still see the players well enough, and I'll feel more comfortable using my binoculars without being noticed from this distance.

I'm surprised to see Greg sitting on the bench while most of his teammates are in the field. Maybe he's having another bad day. Or maybe after yesterday the coach decided he needed to bench him at the beginning of practice to send him and the rest of the team a message: we're preparing for the playoffs, I expect everyone to do their best, and if you don't, look what happens.

I guess it works. As soon as I settle in, the coach sits down and talks to Greg. A pep talk, probably, with the coach using his hands a lot and Greg nodding in constant agreement. Once they're finished, Greg jumps up and runs out to take over his position at third base.

Greg may be doing better than he did yesterday, only missing a couple of ground balls early and making all his throws, but he's not vocal like the rest of the team. He tries, but I can tell his heart's not in it. Using the binoculars, I see a look of fierce determination on his face. He's trying to act like the friendly, outgoing, good sportsmanship guy everybody loves, but something's different. It doesn't look like he's having fun.

This goes on for over half an hour. When all the players finally come in to the bench, I breathe a sigh of relief that practice is over, but it's not. Now everyone is getting ready to hit. This goes on for another half hour. It's so boring. Greg gets in a few decent hits during his turns. When everyone finally gathers at the dugout, I figure, hitting, fielding, that's it. Nothing left, right? But then the coach talks to them. And I mean, for a long time. I get up and stretch. It's approaching an hour and a half.

A good investigator knows when to be patient.

After taking a drink, I'm putting one of the water bottles I brought with me back into my backpack when a new group of players appear, coming from the school parking lot. They must be the junior varsity. Maybe it's their turn to practice. Until I see that the varsity team isn't leaving. They seem to be getting ready to play, and I realize they're going to play each other.

As the varsity team takes the field, I consider taking a break and walking to the nearby Dairy Queen for a milkshake. But I've got to stay here. Keep my eye on Greg. You never know what could happen. And I've got plenty of snacks with me.

A good investigator is always prepared for long stakeouts.

The JV team goes down one, two, three in the first, and Greg and his teammates are getting ready to bat when my cell phone buzzes. Charlie's name is on the screen.

"I told you not to call me!" I snap into the phone.

"No you didn't," Charlie says back.

"I…" I hesitate. She's right. I didn't. "Well, what if I'd been hiding really close to him, and my phone going off gave me away?"

"Did it?"

"No."

"Good," Charlie says. "And you had your phone on vibrate, right?"

"Yeah."

"So everything's copacetic."

"What do you want?" I ask.

"I want to know how it's going."

"It's going fine," I tell her, irritation still in my voice.

"What's he doing?"

"Right at the moment?" The smack of wood makes me look toward the field. "He just got a hit. Looks like it's going to be a double."

"They're still doing baseball practice?"

"Yeah, please shoot me now."

"So he's doing better than he did yesterday?"

"Yeah. Looks like a talk from his coach helped."

"Do you think he told him, 'Don't let a little murder ruin your game, play your best. For the team?'"

"I think he's acting like he's got something heavy on his mind, but he's doing his best to play through it."

"Do you want me to come join you?"

"No," I say after thinking about it. "It's still better if I do this alone."

"You sure?" Again, she sounds disappointed. "I'm the one who got you the backpack. Heck, I'm the one who found the cross."

"I still think it's better."

"I've got news," Charlie says with a new lift to her voice.

"News?"

"While you've been sitting on your butt watching a bunch of jocks, I've been doing investigative work of my own."

"What do you mean?" I say, feeling suddenly wary.

"I got to thinking, how difficult can it be to learn the name of the church camp Amy's supposed to be attending this weekend? Find out if she's there or not. I mean to confirm it."

"Charlie, what did you do?" My voice comes out sharp and raspy.

"Don't worry, it was easy."

"What was?"

"This guy who works out when I do—"

"What guy?"

"Just a guy, his name's Jason, he's a year older than us, a senior, you probably don't know him. Come on, let me finish my story."

I wait, the fingers of my left hand tapping on my backpack.

"He works out at school at a lot of the times I'm there," Charlie continues. "He and I are friendly."

"'Friendly,' huh?"

"You jealous?"

Before I can come up with an answer, she says, "He dates one of Amy's friends. I know where he works out on Sundays, and I caught him there. I asked him some questions—"

"What kinds of questions?"

"Chill, I kept it normal. Just asked him about this church camp I heard Amy Sloan had gone to. That I'd heard it was kind of strict. He said his girlfriend told him it's super religious, shocker. They want the campers to focus so they really don't let them keep their cell phones. He knew the name of the camp. Actually, I realized if we'd asked the reverend, he probably would have told us, duh. Anyway, I looked it up online. And called."

"You...you called it?"

"Yeah, it was no big deal. I asked for Amy, the woman who answered said campers could not get calls unless it was an emergency.

I was about to go into this big thing saying it wasn't an emergency, but it was *really* important—"

"Charlie—"

"Will you stop interrupting me?" she blurts out. "I didn't have to make up anything. Before I could, she says, 'I can see she's not here.'"

I think my heart stops. "What?"

"The woman says Amy never checked in. She has a list of those who did, and her name's not checked. She's not there, Alden."

"Because she's dead," I hear myself whisper.

I'm sitting outside, the sun is bright and uncovered by clouds, and yet I feel a deep chill. Everything seems to be closing in around me. I look at the field below. The players are running, throwing, catching, cheering, and encouraging each other, like everything's normal, like the world didn't just take a giant, awful turn.

"Alden, you there?" I hear from the phone.

"Yeah," I say after a moment.

"This is getting real now. I think part of me was hoping it would turn out she'd been at camp all along."

She pauses as if expecting me to say something, but I don't. There's another crack of the bat; the varsity players cheer as it clears the center-field fence. My mind is numb as I watch Greg trot home from second base before turning to thump his teammate's back after he crosses home plate.

My eyes start to burn.

"We need to stop," Charlie says.

"Stop?" I mumble.

"We need to tell my father."

I remain silent. The quiet stretches until Charlie asks, "Alden? Did you hear me?"

"No."

"I said we need to—"

"I mean, no, we can't tell him yet."

There's a pause before Charlie says, "We can't keep quiet about this any longer. We've got to tell him."

"We will. But I want to keep following Greg a little longer."

"Why, what would that accomplish?"

"I might get more evidence."

"We don't *need* any more evidence. She's not at the camp. You saw him beat her to death. We have his backpack with her blood on it. We have her cross that we found at the place she was killed. What more do we need?"

"Maybe he'll…" I hesitate.

"Maybe he'll what?" Charlie almost shouts. "Lead you to a plot of ground with a sign that says 'Amy Sloan is Buried Here After I Murdered Her, signed Greg Matthes?'"

"No," I say, amazed on some level by how I'm able to keep myself under control. "No sign. But he still might lead me to a place the police could check out. Hopefully find her body."

"It's not our job anymore, Alden. It's the police's job. My dad needs to know"

"Or maybe…" I stop myself.

"Maybe what?"

When I don't say anything, Charlie says, "Oh, I get it. You're hoping she's still alive and you can save her. Maybe Greg didn't kill her, he just hurt her, and he's holding her prisoner somewhere, and you're hoping you'll swoop in and save her. And then she'll be so happy, and everyone will think you're a hero and—"

"Charlie!" I snap.

"What!" she snaps back.

I open my mouth to reply, but nothing comes out. A part of me is wondering if she's right.

"I'm sorry for what I just said," Charlie says. "It was…" She hesitates. "But this isn't a game, Alden."

"I never said it was." Then I hear myself say, "We could do it anonymously. Like before."

Charlie doesn't respond.

"We call the police," I continue. "*I* call them. Tell them what happened. Then I hang up. Like before."

"What about the backpack and the cross?"

"We can leave it for them somewhere to find. Then we're done with it. But give me the rest of the day. To see if I find something more."

"What if he *is* just holding her prisoner somewhere, and there's still time to—"

"She's dead, Charlie. You know it, and I do, too. Give me the rest of the day to find something I can really nail Greg with."

"You'll call me tonight?" Charlie says after a moment.

"Yes."

"And whether you learn anything more by tonight or not, we still tell the police."

"Yes. And one more thing."

"What?" Charlie says, sounding wary.

"It looks like this is going to take longer than I thought. Uncle Bill will be wondering where I am when he gets home. When he calls me I'm going to tell him I'm with you, working on an important homework assignment. He won't call you, but if necessary, can you back me up?"

"Yeah. Okay," Charlie agrees. Suddenly, she says, "My parents are home. Gotta go!" I hear her saying, "Hi, Mom. Hi, Dad," before she ends the call.

I slip my phone back into my pocket and turn my attention back to the players. The varsity seems to be crushing junior varsity. The JV pitcher has his head down as another varsity player rounds the bases in another home run trot. The JV coach walks out to the pitcher's mound where the rest of the team also gathers. He says something to the pitcher before giving him a pat on the shoulder.

The infielders pat him on the back or give him words of encouragement that I can't make out, but the pitcher still walks off dejectedly. It's just a game, I want to shout at him. Not even an important game, a scrimmage. It doesn't mean anything!

The rest of the game plays out in a kind of blur, until the JV team finally calls uncle after five innings. Through the binoculars, my eyes stay glued to Greg as he joins his teammates in listening to the coach. To me he looks troubled and anxious, but nobody seems to notice.

I notice. Because I know his secret.

And soon others are going to know, too. So keep playing your stupid baseball. Like it matters. It's not going to matter tomorrow. Not baseball or the playoffs or anything, because all anybody is going to be talking about is Greg Matthes, the murderer.

A good investigator does not let his emotions get in the way of his investigation.

I take a deep breath to calm myself down.

The players finally break and head off in various directions. Two guys I don't really know but whose names I remember as Nick and Riley walk with him. I stay back for a couple of minutes, letting them gain some distance as they walk away before I hoist my backpack up onto my shoulder and begin following them.

There's a strong feeling of power gained from following another person, in knowing that the person has no idea you're watching.

People are so into their own stuff, not seeing what's around them, much less someone following them, that sometimes they end up revealing something only you are privy to. But it's important not to let that power go to your head. You get too cocky and you can get too close. Make a mistake. Keeping your distance from the person being pursued while keeping your wits about you and staying observant makes you invisible, not only to the one you're following, but to everyone else you pass on the way.

I settle into a steady pace behind Greg and his friends. My gaze is as focused as it has ever been. My instincts are razor sharp. And Greg and the other two guys aren't paying attention. Nick and Riley are talking back and forth as if involved in a friendly argument. Greg seems distracted, throwing in an occasional comment but mostly just walking, lost in his own thoughts.

The three go inside a convenience store, and I step into a bookstore across the street, checking out the books on display near the front window until I see them coming out with bottles of Gatorade in hand, and they keep walking and talking and not noticing me. At times, it feels as if I could pick up my pace and get close enough to touch them, and still they wouldn't know I was there. I resist the urge and keep my pace steady.

Eventually they reach a corner where Greg breaks off from the other two and, waving, heads off in a different direction. I pull back a little so Riley and Nick are farther away, and there's little chance they'll see me before I turn my attention to Greg. Now that he is alone, he picks up his pace, moving much faster, his head down. It's as if he is trying to get away from something. Maybe from himself. From his crime.

I'm far enough behind him I feel safe increasing my own pace. But soon it becomes clear he's just going home. Once he reaches the front of his house, he turns down the path leading up to the front door, opens it, and quickly goes inside.

He didn't have to unlock the door to go inside, which probably means at least some of his family are home. I settle onto the same bench I was sitting on yesterday. This time I don't pull anything out of my backpack to make it look like I'm doing something innocuous. I just keep my gaze fixed on the Matthes house. Staring, not moving, as if I want Greg to look out a window and see me watching him. Telling him with my eyes, I know what you've done, Greg. I know.

This is getting real now.

My phone buzzes, and for a quick moment I think it's Greg calling because he's seen me and wants to know what the hell I'm doing.

He wouldn't have my cell phone number, though, and pulling my phone out of my pocket, I see the name on the phone screen and push the answer button. "Hi, Uncle Bill."

"I'm home, and I've already ordered the pizza. Pepperoni *and* sausage *and* extra cheese." He sounds much more upbeat than usual, even jovial. "Where are you?"

"I'm with Charlie," I lie. "We're working on a really important homework assignment that I kind of let slide. I don't know how long it'll take for us to finish."

A beat. Then, "Oh." The disappointment in his voice catches me by surprise. "I was hoping we'd…" He doesn't finish his sentence but it's enough for a pang of guilt to begin gnawing in my stomach. I quickly push it down. My eyes stay glued to the Matthes house.

"Do you know how long it will take?" he asks. "I could call back and get them to delay the order."

"It could be pretty late," I tell him. "It's a really big assignment. I shouldn't have put it off."

"Okay," he says after a moment. "No problem." There's another long pause. "It'll be here when you get home. You can just heat it up."

An awkward silence follows. I open my mouth, not sure what I'm going to say when my uncle says, "You better get back to work, Alden. Keep those grades up. Don't be working too late, though…" His voice trails off.

"Sure," I say.

"Okay then. Bye."

"Bye."

He hangs up, and I lay the phone down carefully next to me on the bench. I feel bad, but this is too important. I have to stay vigilant.

A few lights come on in the Matthes house. Other than that, I don't see much sign of movement. I wonder what he's doing in there, what he's thinking.

More time passes.

A good investigator is always patient. But ready for anything.

Eventually, I pull out a book of crossword puzzles I keep in my backpack. With half of my attention on the book, the other half on the house across the street, I hunker down and wait for something to happen.

SEVENTEEN

Before the shooting started, I was standing in line with Charlie to buy a snow cone. I'd always enjoyed going to the annual fair since the town of Milton started it when Charlie and I were seven. We were both in good moods that day, our hair mussed after having ridden a few of the fair rides, saving the zip line for last. But I couldn't spend the day at the fair without a snow cone. Or two or three.

"Soft-serve ice cream is better," Charlie was saying.

"Nope," I said, a grin on my face. This argument was a yearly ritual, a game we played—maybe this year she was finally going to give in and get a snow cone.

"A snow cone is just crushed, flavored ice." Charlie countered. "Soft serve is smooth and delicious, and a lot easier to eat."

"Soft serve is very good," I continued. "But when you're at a fair, you've got to have a snow cone. It's only natural."

"Natural," Charlie scoffed, but with a grin on her face as well. "What does that mean?" This summer her long brown arms had really started to show the results of the weight lifting she'd started doing. "Ice cream is better period, fair or no fair."

"I do not agree," I said laughing. "And how would you know? You've never even had a snow cone."

"Yes, I have," she insisted.

"When?"

"When I was six. Bubble gum, that disgusting flavor you like. It made me throw up."

I shook my head. "It did not."

"Yep, it sure did."

"That was ten years ago. You'd probably like it now."

She made a face. "You sound like my mother."

"She thinks you should try a snow cone?"

"No, brussels sprouts."

"Oh. Well, still…"

"Do you like brussels sprouts?"

How did we start talking about vegetables? "No."

"Did you like them when you were six?"

"No."

"I rest my case." She brushed her hands together, like it was a done deal.

"It's not the same thing."

"How is it different?"

"You don't have to have bubble gum. You can have another flavor."

"All the flavors suck."

We went on like that as the line got smaller. Some people probably thought we were having a real fight, but we weren't. This was fun. We could argue about anything. After bingeing the original *Twilight Zone*, we argued over which was the best episode. Then after bingeing Rod Serling's other show, we argued over which episodes of *Night Gallery* were good enough to be in *Twilight Zone* and which ones weren't. Sometimes Charlie could get into it a bit too much, but not that day at the fair. That day she was funny and teasing. I had known her all my life, had grown up with her, but, for the first time, I was noticing how beautiful she was. How great her smile was, and how much her deep-blue eyes lit up when she laughed. For the first time, I was wondering what she would say if, after we got our snow cones and took a walk to eat them, I asked her if I could kiss her.

We were only one customer away from being served, the closest she'd ever gotten, when Charlie blurted out, "Nope, I can't."

"Sure you can," I said. "Look, you're almost there."

"My taste buds are screaming for ice cream. Besides, you don't want me to throw up on you, do you?"

"You won't throw up. I promise."

She cupped her ear. "I hear it calling to me. Here I come, ice cream! I'm coming to eat you."

"Charlie…" I said, but I was laughing, and leaning in, she said, "When you're lying on the ground, sick and dying from the snow cone you just ate, remember, you could have had soft serve with me." Then she surprised me with a kiss on the cheek, and before I could react, she was running off in the opposite direction.

The spot where she'd kissed me was burning as I placed my hand against it, as if it to keep it there for as long as I could, until the man serving behind the stand leaned out and said, "Hey, Romeo, you want a snow cone or not?"

After stepping out of line and taking several delicious mouthfuls of sweet bubble gum ice, I saw my mom and dad not too far away. They saw me and waved, and I waved back, intending to go find Charlie when Dad motioned me to come over.

"Having fun?" Dad asked when I reached them.

I nodded, my mouth full.

"Where's Charlie?" Mom asked.

"She's getting ice cream. I'm going to go meet up with her. After we finish, we're going to ride the zip line."

"Before you go," Dad said, "we have something to tell you. Good news I think you'll really like."

"What?" I asked.

I remember Dad placed his hand on my shoulder, and the

smiles on both his and Mom's faces were so big, whatever it was had to be really good.

But before he could tell me, his expression changed. One minute he was smiling, the next his eyes widened, and before I knew what was happening, he shouted, "*Get down!*" He grabbed me, my snow cone flying out of my hand, and he was trying to cover me with his body while pushing me to the ground, only I didn't go down, not at first; I got tangled in my own feet as I heard one shot ring out, then another, and he let go of me, as if something had yanked his hand away. I tried to get my balance before more shots sounded, louder than before, and people began to yell, then scream, then finally gravity won out and, like a marionette with its strings cut, I started to fall.

EIGHTEEN

The sky has started to darken when I see one of the garage doors opening, and a car pulls out with Greg's mom and sister. That leaves only Greg's dad in there with him, though I haven't seen him, so I can't be sure. I'd moved to a different spot in the park, sitting on the grass, my back against a tree, but I can still see the Matthes house clearly. The park is empty, and has been for the last hour, so there's no one to question what I'm doing.

I stopped doing crosswords over an hour ago, content to just watch even though nothing much has happened. All I know is Greg could have incriminating evidence I'm not aware of yet. I don't know what, but something.

Or maybe there's nothing more to find, and I'm wasting my time. Truth is, I'm not getting much done. And it's looking like Greg is staying in for the night.

I should get moving. Go home. A good investigator may need

to be thorough and patient, but big homework assignment or no big homework assignment, Uncle Bill is going to start wondering. I'm not going to learn anything more tonight.

Charlie is right. We need to tell her father. Get the police involved.

Time to go.

My cell phone rings. Not my uncle; it's Charlie.

"I haven't learned anything new," I say into the phone. "I'm going to—"

"Get back here," Charlie hisses into my ear.

"Get back where? Your house?"

"I'm in the Mattheses' backyard. Behind the shed."

I almost drop my phone. "You're *where?*"

"Shhh, keep your voice down."

"Why... How did you... I'm across the street. I can see the front of the house. I didn't see you."

"I climbed over the back fence, from the property behind theirs. Will you hurry up and get over here?"

I hang up and grab my backpack. I consider getting into their yard the same way Charlie did, but that would take longer. Charlie made it clear I need to get over there as quick as I can.

Taking in a deep breath, I run across the street to the same fence door I'd used yesterday, twice. The door makes a timid screech as I open it, and my heart feels like it stops. I listen, hear nothing. My phone buzzes, and I look down to see a text from Charlie: **RUN NOW!**

Another breath and I take off through the backyard, praying Greg isn't looking out his back window. When I make it to the shed, Charlie's arm suddenly appears and yanks me out of sight of the house. Losing my balance, I fall to the ground. On hands and knees, I take a minute to get my breath.

"You took long enough," I hear Charlie say.

"What if…what if he saw me?" I manage.

"He didn't. He's not in his room. But he will be shortly."

"What are you doing here?"

"I was getting antsy waiting to hear from you," Charlie says. "I figured you could use some help. I decided to take a chance that you'd ended up at his house. When I saw you across the street, I figured I'd be more useful back here."

"You saw me?"

"Course I did. You weren't all that hidden. I'm sure Greg hasn't seen you, though."

"How long have you been back here?"

She shrugs. "About a half hour." She points toward the house. "He's been in his room most of the time."

"Why didn't you call me?"

"You'd already made it pretty clear you didn't want me to."

"What about your mom and dad?"

"They think I'm studying with you. You got me through math, remember? They're never going to give me a hard time about you and I studying together."

"But what if they call my house and my uncle tells them—"

"They'd call my cell phone first, you know that. Listen. He's been looking for his backpack."

"What?"

"He's frantic. Looked inside his closet, took a lot of stuff out of there, didn't find it. Then he started tearing up his room. No luck, of course." Suddenly, she points. "Hey, he's back."

I see Greg through the window, walking into his room carrying what looks like a dark-green garbage bag.

"I knew it!" Charlie exclaims.

"Knew what?"

"Look."

Greg picks up clothes and shoves them into the bag. A shirt, a pair of jeans, a light tan jacket that looks familiar, a belt, white socks, and even a pair of sneakers.

"How much you want to bet those are the clothes he was wearing when you saw him kill Amy?" Charlie says. "Probably has blood on them, so he's getting rid of them."

My gaze returns to the window. "Why does he still have them?" I say.

"Because he's no great criminal mind. Maybe he thought he

could wash them, but the blood wouldn't come out. Like with his backpack. Now he's finally given in and wants to get rid of all of it. Look."

Now he's emptying a trash can into the bag. He leaves the room for a moment then comes back, the bag looking heavier. Must be more trash in there to mix in with the incriminating clothing.

He puts the bag down and, putting his hands on his hips, looks around the room. For a moment or two he doesn't move. At one point he seems to look out the window, and my instinct is to pull back. But I quickly realize he's not peering out.

Then he walks into his open closet. "He's looking again," Charlie utters as he steps out of view. "Hoping he just missed it somehow."

He's back in a couple of minutes, a fresh look of distress on his face. He moves to the window, and this time we both pull back. He stares out for several seconds before turning away.

"I guess he realizes he should have thrown away the backpack earlier. But it's too late now." She gives a sinister-sounding chuckle.

"What do you think he's going to do?" I ask.

"Well, he might think his parents found it and will confront him about it. So he'll try to come up with a story to explain the blood. It'll be hard to convince them it's his, since he doesn't have any sign of a wound on him." Charlie thinks for a moment. "Actually, I don't know what he'll do."

Then, in a soft voice, she says, "We've got you, sucker."

Greg is not moving and seems to be thinking.

"Now what?" I say.

"He probably wants to search the rest of the house, but he can't, not with his dad home," Charlie speculates.

"Or maybe he's figured out somebody else besides his parents has it," I say.

"Maybe. But there's no way to know it's us."

I think back to returning here last night to look for my notebook, but decide not to say anything.

"Get ready to move," Charlie says. I look at the window; Greg's tying up the trash bag. "As soon as he leaves his room, run with me to the fence door."

Greg glances around his room one more time, as if the backpack might suddenly reappear out of thin air. When he finally leaves, we take off, running to the fence. Charlie pauses only a second before she undoes the latch, and we slip through to the front of the house, no screech this time.

"Quick, over here," I tell her, remembering the bushes I'd hid behind in the neighbors' yard last night. I lead the way, the two of us crouching down just in time as Greg comes out of the front door, tied-up bag in hand.

Clearly, trash pickup is tomorrow, what with all the trash cans sitting by the curb up and down the street. Greg walks to the can in front of his house, grabs the top of the cover, then hesitates, looking around at the other trash cans lining the street.

"He's realizing it might be too risky to throw the clothes away in their own trash can," Charlie whispers. "He's wondering if he can get away with tossing it into one of his neighbors' containers."

Greg tries to look casual as he begins to walk away from us down the sidewalk, toward other trash cans. "Pay attention to what can he picks," Charlie orders.

All at once, headlights appear from around the block. Greg stops, then makes an abrupt turn back toward us. The headlights slow, and I realize the car is preparing to turn into the Mattheses' driveway. Greg's mother and sister returning home.

"Too late," Charlie says, sounding downright gleeful. "He couldn't very well explain to his mother why he was throwing away trash in his neighbor's can. Bad for him, easier for us."

The headlights illuminate Greg just as he reaches his family's trash can and opens the lid.

Reaching in, he pulls out two bags that were already in there, drops the bag he'd brought out into the can, then drops the other bags on top of it. Replacing the lid, he turns and waves as his mother's car passes him in the driveway, then, with a quick glance back at the trash can, he walks to the front door of the house. There, like a good son, he waits for them to come out of the garage.

Greg asks his sister, "How'd it go?" I don't make out her answer as they all go into the house.

Neither Charlie or I move for about a minute. Then Charlie whispers into my ear, "Let's go!"

Quickly, we dart out from behind the bush and run to the trash can. Charlie yanks open the lid, and I reach in and pull out the two top bags. Charlie pulls out the bag we want, and I toss the other two back in. We run across the street and into the playground.

We crouch down, and Charlie unties the bag.

"What if Greg comes back out later to move the bag to one of his neighbors' cans like he planned?" I ask.

"He won't. Too much risk now that his entire family's home." Charlie looks into the bag. "Ta-daaa," she calls out, pulling out a shirt. "Notice the telltale bloodstain." The sky has settled into night, so I turn on the flashlight app on my phone. The beam allows us to make out the splash of brown on the front.

"How come it's not red?" I ask Charlie.

"Spilled blood like this changes color after time," she answers.

Blood can also be found on the jeans at the belt loops and more on the belt itself. We find some near the zipper of the jacket as well, a small amount, but enough that Greg decided to chuck it. There's blood on the sneakers, too, and even the socks. We stare at the clothing laid out in front of us in silence. Seeing Amy's blood on Greg's clothes like this feels somehow different than finding it on his backpack, even if it was the murder weapon. Her blood on Greg's clothing makes it feel more sobering, more intimate. More real than it already did.

Charlie lets out a big sigh. "We better get this over to your house."

We start walking. By the time we're in sight of my house, we have a plan in place for tomorrow.

"We could get all the evidence and take it to my dad right now," Charlie says.

I let out a tired sigh. "It's late."

"He won't care with something as important as this."

"Come on, Charlie, I'm tired, I want to go to sleep. Let's stick to the plan. Do it tomorrow. Anonymously. It's better he doesn't know it came from us."

"Our DNA is on the evidence, too, you know."

That makes me hesitate. "We'll cross that bridge if we have to."

I can tell Charlie wants to say more, but she stops and just nods.

"I'll call you tomorrow after I've done it," I tell her.

Charlie waves and heads off in the direction of her house.

Glancing through the front window, I see Uncle Bill asleep in his usual spot. Moving carefully, I make it up to my room without waking him. After stuffing the bag of Greg's clothes into the far corner of my closet, I walk quietly downstairs and into the kitchen. More than half the pizza sits in its box on the kitchen table. I consider heating up a couple of pieces, but I end up just wrapping the pieces in tin foil and putting them in the refrigerator.

I stare at my uncle, his mouth partway open, breathing heavily. He'd seemed excited about getting to spend time with me, eating my favorite pizza, and I consider waking him. But today had been a big day, and tomorrow was going to be even bigger, and, ultimately I'm just too tired. Leaving him asleep in his chair, I trudge upstairs.

I tumble tiredly into bed, but can't fall asleep, my mind racing. It's actually a fairly simple plan, and once I've completed it, I'll wash my hands of the case. Charlie's dad and his officers can take over. Arrest Greg and throw him in jail for what he's done. Maybe once Greg sees all the evidence the police are about to get from me, he'll confess and it'll all be over.

Uncle Bill stirs downstairs. By the time he turns off the TV and comes upstairs, I've turned away and closed my eyes. I sense him pause in the doorway, looking in on me. Maybe I hear him softly say my name to see if I'm still awake, but I don't respond, don't move.

After a couple of minutes, he sighs and walks down the hall to his bedroom.

I toss and turn for a long time after that, but eventually, I fall into a troubled sleep.

NINETEEN

Despite a night of restless sleep, I'm ready to go. I know it's mostly nervous adrenaline that's energizing me, and later today I'll probably crash, but for now, I'm okay. I find a note from Uncle Bill sitting on the kitchen table. It reads: *Sorry, but I have to be at work even earlier than usual all this week. Hope you got your assignment finished last night. If I can help, let me know. See you tonight.*

I hate lying to him.

He left out cereal for me, but my stomach is too tied up in knots to eat anything.

Last night, I attached each piece of evidence with a note explaining its significance before returning it to the bag: Inside a clear sandwich bag, the cross necklace that Amy never goes anywhere without found at the scene of the crime. The backpack used to kill her when there were books in it, with her blood on it. The smaller bag containing the clothing worn by Greg when he killed her, also with Amy's blood on them. Even the trash he'd put in with the clothes. Finally, a typed letter explaining exactly what I saw that day at Miller's Park. A letter I left unsigned.

With any luck, this will be enough to make Greg confess his crime, and the police won't have to know my identity. But I've thought about it now, and if this is not enough, and I have to reveal myself in order to testify, then so be it. I will. If that happens, I will not mention Charlie's name or her involvement in this, DNA or no DNA. I haven't told her that, but my mind is made up. If not coming forward sooner turns out to be a problem, then it will fall on me. Not Charlie.

Grabbing the bag, I go outside, glancing around to see if anybody is watching me before closing the front door.

The plan Charlie and I devised is simple. It's also the best we could come up with.

It turns out Charlie had been thinking ahead to this particular situation and had bought a burner phone, the kind with only a certain amount of call time available on them and not connected to any name, if you don't want it to be. The plan is I'll use it to make only one call, then I'll throw it away. The police will show up, find the bag where I told them it'd be, and that'll be it. My job as private detective will be finished. Case closed. I'll get to school just in time for the first period bell to ring.

Charlie had wanted to do something to help, but I'd convinced her it was best done by one person, and that person was me. All she had to do was go to school as usual and act surprised when her dad showed up to arrest Greg Matthes.

The place we chose to leave the bag was where the old strip mall used to be. I try to take a route that has as few people as possible. The ones I do pass don't seem to pay any attention to me. Once I get there, I place the bag behind the old sandwich shop. A red ribbon flutters around the neck of the bag—a sign I devised to let the police know what to look for.

I find a spot across the street where I can see the bag from behind a wire fence and not be easily seen. Taking a deep breath, I call the police station—not 911 like last time, but the main number.

"Milton Police Department. Officer Mallory speaking."

I open my mouth, and, at first, I'm afraid my voice isn't going to work. And then it all comes pouring out. "Amy Sloan was killed last Friday afternoon after school by Greg Matthes at Miller's Park. The reason the police didn't find her body was because he moved it. No one knows she's missing because they thought she was away at church camp. But—"

"Just a minute," the voice on the other end says. "Who is—"

"I've left the proof you need behind what used to be Amos's Sandwich Shop on Pell Street," I continue. "A bag with a red ribbon. It's there now. Please hurry."

I hang up and shove the cell into my pants pocket. Better I throw it away someplace far from here.

According to the plan, I should be walking to school now. But there's something else I didn't tell Charlie: I'd decided this morning I wasn't going to leave right after the call. I need to stay here, hidden, to make sure the police find the bag. What if I leave and there's a mix-up? Like the police officer I spoke to not getting the bag's location right. Or someone else wanders by before the police arrive, sees the bag, and takes it. It's risky, I know, but I need to make sure things go as planned.

I'm sure only minutes go by, but they feel like hours. How long does it take for the police to get here? Milton is not that big. Is it possible the officer didn't believe me? Maybe he thinks it's another prank, so they're not coming.

No, they're the police. They can't let something like this go without at least checking it out.

I keep waiting. A guy comes into view a couple blocks away and keeps walking until he stops near where I left the bag. I raise up on my haunches. He's only stopped to light a cigarette, thank God. He tosses the used match then moves on. That would be just great if his careless match caught the bag on fire, but after a minute I see no sign of flames.

More time passes. Still nothing. My left leg is starting to hurt. I shift position. Should I call again?

A siren blares in the distance, growing louder. I didn't think about the police using a siren, but of course they would, something as important as this. My whole body shakes in anticipation—and when I think about it, fear.

They're almost here. I won't leave until I'm sure they've actually found it.

I shift my position again. The siren is getting louder.

My cell phone buzzes. Not the burner cell still in my pocket. My cell.

Charlie's name pops up on the screen. "Why are you—?"

"Don't make the call!" Her voice is frantic.

"What? I—"

"*Did* you make the call?"

Something hard and cold forms in my stomach. "Yes. A few minutes ago."

"Oh crap, oh shit!"

Charlie never curses. "What's going on?" I ask her, a painful thrum starting in my chest.

"She's not dead."

There's a ringing in my ears that has nothing to do with the sirens. "What?"

"Greg didn't kill Amy."

I open my mouth, but nothing comes out.

"I just saw her. She's here at school."

The ringing is drowned out by the actual police siren. Not far now.

"Amy Sloan is *alive!*"

TWENTY

Before the shooting started, before standing in line with Charlie for snow cones, I remember the two of us getting off the Tilt-a-Whirl, holding on to each other to get our balance.

"That was fun," Charlie said.

"That was dangerous," I countered.

"Danger's part of the fun."

"Did you feel how rickety it was? I thought we were going to fly off the track." My stomach was still a little queasy.

"Like I said. Danger is part—"

"We should report that ride to your father. I'll bet it hasn't been inspected since our parents were our age."

"Well, look at you, acting like a crybaby."

I pull back. "Crybaby?"

"Sorry. I meant wimp."

"Oh yeah?" I can see her fighting to keep from laughing. I'm doing the same.

"Is that all you can say?"

I gave her a playful push. She laughed and pushed me back, almost knocking me off my feet, and she grabbed my arm to steady me.

Her fingers on my skin, even if it was just to stop me from falling on my butt, sent a tingle shooting through me. We've been friends for forever, but I'd been noticing that tingle more and more lately. Was I just imagining her holding on to me a little longer than necessary before letting go?

"This is the year you said you'd do the zip line," Charlie commanded. "I say we do that one next."

"Did I say that? I don't remember saying that."

"You did. You're not gonna wimp out on me now, are you?"

"What, did you just learn that word yesterday?"

"We're doing the zip line next."

"First we get a snow cone."

Before she had a chance to object, I added, "Or are you going to wimp out?"

That stopped her. She frowned at me. "As I remember, I promised I'd stand in the snow cone line with you."

In a singsong voice, I said, "Wimp, wimp, wimpy wimp…"

"All right, all right," she said, laughing. Something else I'd been noticing lately: how much I enjoyed her laugh. "I'll get in line with you. Then the zip line. But first I gotta pee."

"You're not going to run out on me, are you?" I jeered as she turned toward one of the lines of temporary Porta Potties set up about a hundred yards away.

"Stay here and find out for yourself." Then off she went. I found myself staring at her long, muscled legs as she ran. Something in the way she moved screamed confidence. And grace. I couldn't believe I'd never realized that about her before.

Self-consciously I turned away, inadvertently stepping into the path of someone trying to walk past me. A man moving quickly, with his head down, wearing a jacket that seemed too heavy for the hot day. His arms were wrapped around his waist as if he was holding something in. All this I took in just before we collided, the man letting out a *woomf* sound. We both came close to falling but managed to stay upright. Still, he dropped something—a brown paper bag with something inside it lying on the ground.

"I'm sorry," I said and reached for the bag, my fingers taking hold. I started to pick it up, intent on giving it to him.

"I've got it!" the man barked, roughly shoving me aside, the bag and its contents falling from my grasp. For less than a second, I saw the edge of something peek out before he had it in his hand and straightened up, shoving the bag back into his jacket.

"I'm sorry," I said again. "I didn't mean to—"

"Asshole," the man grumbled. Surprised, I backed off, and he retreated, hunched over as if afraid the bag would fall out of his jacket again.

I stared as he walked away. Though I hadn't seen what was in the bag, I'd felt it, for the second or so I'd had my fingers around it. The way he was protecting it now bothered me.

"Miss me?" Charlie popped up beside me, giving me a nudge.

"Did you see that guy?" I said.

"What guy?" But she wasn't looking.

"That guy over there," I said, pointing.

She followed my finger. "What guy are you talking about?"

He was too far away now. "We bumped into each other," I told her. "He dropped something, and when I tried to pick it up for him, he got all defensive about it. Shoved me out of the way to get it."

"So what was it?"

"I don't know. I just barely touched it. Why would he be so weird about it?"

Charlie shrugged. "Who knows?"

"Where's your dad?" I asked suddenly, looking around.

She shrugged again, glancing around half-heartedly. "I don't know. People bump into each other all the time. Is there something else he did?"

"He called me an asshole."

"Oh, by all means then, let's find my dad. That's a jailable offense. A life sentence."

When I didn't respond, Charlie said, "You're just delaying getting on the zip line."

The guy was completely out of sight. Charlie was probably right. It was nothing. "All right, let's go."

Charlie pointed. "The zip line is off in that direction."

"Uh-uh," I said. "Snow cones first."

A couple of minutes later, I was in line bantering back and forth with Charlie, anticipating a bubble-gum-flavored snow cone, no longer thinking about the strange guy I'd bumped into. Until six people had been shot, and I saw him again, dead on the ground, a gun by his side.

TWENTY-ONE

"We should never have let it get this far," Charlie moans.

We've been here five minutes, and that's the first thing she's said. We'd decided it was best not to talk about it at school. I've waited on pins and needles all day. We walked to my house, saying nothing along the way. Since we've gotten here, Charlie has done nothing but pace the living room, wearing an expression on her face that says shut up, I'm thinking.

So I've just been sitting and watching her—and waiting. I may be able to read her expression, but I've never seen her this intense. This upset.

She repeats her path across the living room carpet a few more times, then suddenly stops in front of me. "Aren't you going to say anything?" she asks.

My mouth drops open a little. "I've been waiting for you."

She stares at me, then turns away and starts pacing again.

"You want something to drink?" I try.

Her expression turns fierce. "Are you kidding me?"

"No," I say.

"Why are you acting like this is no big deal?"

"I'm not. I just… We need to sit down and talk about this eventually. And I'm thirsty."

I get up and walk into the kitchen. In many ways, this is a duplicate of what happened when I told her what I had seen at Miller's Park. Except our roles are reversed. Now Charlie is the one out of control, and I'm trying to calm *her* down.

Charlie hasn't responded to my question, but I still pull out two ginger ales. Back in the living room, I extend one. She hesitates, then snatches it from my hand. Following my lead, she sits on the couch, emptying half the can in one long gulp.

It clanks on the coffee table. She asks, "The evidence is safe?"

"I've still got it."

"And you're sure the police didn't see you?"

"I'm sure."

Right after Charlie's call, and with the police siren wailing down my neck, I raced out from behind the wire fence, grabbed the bag of evidence, and ran away before they arrived. If I'd taken a minute longer, I would have been caught with the bag in hand. If I'd taken thirty seconds beyond that, I probably would have been seen tossing the bag over the fence. But neither happened.

By the time the police cruiser pulled up to the rear of the old sandwich shop, I was back behind the fence, scrunched down. I recognized the officer as the same one who had given Tommy Zimmerman the ticket in front of Greg Matthes's house a couple days ago. And as soon as she reached where the bag was supposed to be, her back to me, I tore out of there. Slowing down to a fast walk after a couple blocks, I took a different way home and put the evidence back in its hiding place. Then I raced for school, hearing the first period bell ring as I walked into the building. Fortunately, my first class is close to the main door. Maybe a couple of students in the classroom noticed I was out of breath as I walked in, but nobody was staring at me. Everything seemed normal.

Until I saw Police Chief Walker escorting Amy Sloan and Greg Matthes down a hallway filled with surprised, murmuring students. By the end of the day, everyone was talking about the massive prank that had been pulled on the police. And on Amy and Greg.

"You have to get rid of the evidence," Charlie says.

"I will."

"Take it somewhere and burn it. Or throw away each of the things in a different place so they're not found together."

"I thought I'd return the cross to her," I say. "Mail it to her anonymously."

"No."

"Or slip it into her locker through the slats."

Her hands fly up into the air so fast I duck. "Are you crazy? No!"

"But it means a lot to her. You said yourself, she never goes anywhere without it."

"Obviously, I was wrong."

"Maybe—" Charlie glares at me, and I shut my mouth.

I wait a full minute, then say, "Let's talk about it, Charlie. Let's figure it out."

"Figure out why we're such idiots, you mean?"

"We were trying to do the right thing."

"The right thing was minding our own business."

"Charlie, I know what I saw."

She rolls her eyes. "Oh, really. You're *sure* about that?"

I start to respond, then falter. Maybe I deserved that. But still…

"She had a cut on her forehead," I point out. "Looked like it needed a couple stitches."

"Which she said she got at camp," Charlie counters. "I heard she told people she got it walking into a branch out on a hike. That she laughed about it."

Charlie jumps up and paces some more. "Really. How can you be so calm, Alden?"

I'm asking myself that same question. Actually, my chest feels like someone is inside trying to get out using a sledgehammer. But I'm not used to seeing Charlie this stressed out, so I guess I figure somebody's got to stay calm.

At least on the outside.

And we do need to think this through.

When a theory turns out to be wrong, a good investigator takes a fresh look at the evidence.

"Amy says she was at church camp all weekend, right?" I say.

Charlie looks like she just wants to fight rather than answer my question, but after a second, she says, "Yes. I heard her telling some girlfriends."

"So how come when you called the camp, the woman said she wasn't there?"

Another pause. "I was wondering about that myself. The woman I spoke to said Amy wasn't there based on her name not being checked."

I look at her. "So you think it was a clerical error? Amy was really there, her name just didn't get checked?"

Charlie shrugs.

"You would think they'd be more careful," I tell her. "Make sure the list matches up with the actual camper count or something."

"Maybe the woman I spoke to wasn't a counselor. Maybe she was just a secretary or receptionist who works out of the camp office, doesn't deal much with the kids. The counselors see Amy is there, they assume she's been checked off, but really, the secretary didn't. She made a mistake."

"Or," I say, a little light going off in my head, "Amy was late."

Charlie looks at me. "Huh?"

Talking about it like this has helped calm the hammering in my chest. A tingle of excitement takes its place. "She was late because she *was* at Miller's Park."

"You're not making sense," Charlie says. "We know Amy was at camp."

"That doesn't mean she wasn't late. She probably got there after the secretary had left for the day, which is why her name wasn't checked when you called on Sunday."

Charlie thinks about it. "Okay. So?"

"We know Amy and Greg were at the field because I saw them there."

Charlie scowls at me. "So *you* say."

"Are you saying I made it up?"

Charlie crosses her arms.

"*You* found her cross necklace there."

"Yeah, I did."

"So Amy was late to camp because she needed to meet Greg at

Miller's Park first. From what I saw, following him there, he wasn't happy about it. She was probably the one who called him on his phone, making sure he was on the way. But why meet him all the way out there?"

"Because she didn't want anybody to see her," Charlie says. "She was supposed to be on her way to church camp."

"And she knew they'd be arguing," I add. "So she wanted a private place to do it. What were they arguing about?"

"Maybe he was seeing somebody else and she found out."

That brings me up short. "Greg? Cheating?"

Charlie bites her lip. "I've heard a rumor."

"Is it true?" I press.

She seems to be considering it, then says, "Nah. I didn't believe it when I heard it. I still don't. I'm sure there are kids jealous enough to spread rumors. See if they could break them up."

"That sucks."

Charlie shrugs. "I guess Amy could be pregnant, and that's when she told him."

"Pregnant? Amy? I just figured they were…"

"Virgins? Not doing it? What I know of them, I'd say the same thing. But they've been together a long time. How much longer can they just kiss and hold hands?"

I nod my head. "That could've been it. Greg couldn't handle it, he got mad, and he hit her with his backpack full of books."

"But maybe it wasn't as bad as you thought."

"You saw the blood on the backpack. And his clothes. And she was lying on the ground."

"Yeah," Charlie says, her voice suddenly rising. "But the big thing you missed was that she *wasn't dead*. She was alive, and you know this because you saw her *walking around in freaking school today!*"

Charlie puts her hand on her forehead. "Look at me, letting you get me caught up in this again." Abruptly, she steps closer, and now she's towering over me. "Okay, I get it, you needed to make that first call on Friday, but when the police didn't find anything, we should have just let it go. If we'd just waited the weekend, we would have seen on Monday she was fine. But, no, we had to play amateur sleuth. We were going to solve the case. Greg killed Amy, and we had the proof. Except our proof is crap, because that's not what happened."

She leans even closer. "You want to hear my theory? Yes, they had an argument. Why? Who cares, it's none of our business. Maybe he hit her, and that's awful. If someone I was dating did that to me, I'd slug him back and tell him we're finished, get out of my life. But maybe he didn't hit her, did you think of that? What did you really see? You didn't actually see him hit her. You saw her lying on the ground with him holding the backpack. But for all you know, she tripped and hit her head against that dugout wall before falling. We found blood there. Maybe she landed on the book bag and that's how her blood got on it. Maybe all Greg had done when you saw him was pick up the backpack from the ground. Maybe if you hadn't panicked and run away, you would have seen him helping her up, then taking her to a doctor to get stitched up before she went off to camp.

"And maybe they were sorry they had argued, maybe it was their first one. They didn't want anyone to know so Amy decided to lie and say her cut happened at church camp, and Greg decided to get rid of the clothes he was wearing after he couldn't wash the blood off and would have done the same thing with the backpack if we hadn't taken it.

"What does all that prove? Well, it tells us that maybe Greg and Amy aren't as perfect as everyone thinks they are. But it doesn't make Greg a murderer because, hey, guess what? Amy's still alive."

Charlie finally stops ranting. I don't know if it means she's finished though, so I let the silence grow.

She lets out a big sigh. "My dad's not gonna let this go. He's gonna be pissed. With the two calls, not to mention those two other calls you made a while back that didn't pan out, he's gonna think he's got a serial prank caller on his hands. He'll investigate. He'll probably want to talk to every kid in school. He finds out I was part of this, I won't be allowed to see daylight for a year."

"He doesn't have to know," I say cautiously.

"You're right about that," she says. "And he's not going to. This stays between us. Right?"

"Right," I say in a quiet voice.

We revert back to silence. Charlie sits down in the chair Uncle Bill likes to fall asleep in after dinner. If things were different, we'd turn on the TV, put on Netflix, and find a movie to watch or a series we're bingeing. Instead, we just sit here, not looking at each other, until I feel compelled to say, "I'm sorry, Charlie. I really am. I thought we were—"

"Doing the right thing," she finishes for me. "Yeah, I know."

After more silence, she says, "The thing I feel the worst about is how I let myself get sucked in."

"What do you mean, 'sucked in'?" A new sense of unease rises in the pit of my stomach.

"It's like we were playing a game," she says. "Cops and robbers... No. Cops and killers. Amy's someone we see every day at school. We're not friends with her, but we know her. We might say hi to her in the hall. And she's so sweet she makes me cringe sometimes, but I like her. She's a person, Alden. But when we thought Amy had been murdered we turned it into a game. Like Clue. Or like those murder mysteries where people dress up as characters. Only we thought this was real. And we still made it a game. What's even worse... I was having fun. How sick is that?"

Finished, Charlie lapses back into silence. I want to argue with her, but I'm not sure how. I think of how much fun she seemed to be having when she broke into Greg Matthes's house. Had I been doing the same? Maybe trying to prove something?

All at once, Charlie stands up. She reaches for the ginger ale she hasn't touched since drinking half of it. Instead of taking a sip, she just stares at it before placing it back on the coffee table. "I know it's difficult…" She hesitates.

"What's difficult?" A lump is suddenly forming in my throat.

"Your parents. What happened to them."

Now the lump is even bigger.

"I remember watching you at their funeral. You looked sad, but you weren't crying. I was sure you'd want to talk about it. I wanted you to talk to me about it. I wanted to be there for you. But you didn't. Not to me, your best friend. Not to anyone. Instead, you play this stupid game."

I bristle at that. "What do you mean?"

"I know why you do it," Charlie continues. "You tell yourself you weren't able to save your parents. You tell yourself it was your fault. You tell yourself that if you keep an eye on people, stay vigilant, follow them even, you'll be able to stop the next tragedy. But what if you did? What if you saved somebody and everyone thought you were a hero? It wouldn't change anything, would it? Your parents would still be gone, and you would still blame yourself. No matter how many times you do it, it's not going to make the pain go away. And all you're doing is spying on people. That's not right. Everybody has secrets. It's not your place to invade other people's privacy. You don't have the right…we don't have the right…to do that."

She stops. The lump in my throat makes talking difficult, but I manage to get out, "I...I didn't know you felt this way."

"I've told you before you should stop. You even promised me."

I don't have anything to say to that.

Charlie stares at me another moment before she says in a hushed voice, "It's not your fault they died. It's the fault of the creep who killed them."

I want to cut her off. Tell her to stop. It feels like my throat is going to explode.

"Your parents did not die because you didn't recognize that the man had a gun."

"He dropped it, Charlie."

"I know."

"I had it in my hand," I hear myself say, though it seems to be coming from somewhere else.

"You barely touched it," Charlie says. "That's what you told me back then."

"But on some level, I knew something was wrong. Something was off about him."

"You had no way of knowing—"

"I should have been more observant. I could have stopped him, told somebody, told your father."

"You don't know that."

"Yes, I do."

"Alden, I was there, too." Tears hover on the edge of her eyes. "I was the one that told you it was nothing, remember? I've thought about that a lot. I ask myself, what if I had listened to what my best friend was saying instead of being so gung ho about going on that stupid zip line? Maybe—"

She stops. Takes a deep breath. I'm not sure if I want to hug her or tell her to get out.

Charlie gets herself under control before she turns those intense eyes of hers on me and says, "I loved your mom and dad, Alden. They were great people. I miss them, too. What happened was awful. But we don't know what might have happened if we'd reacted differently. We don't. And I refuse to let speculation and what-ifs control my life. And you should do the same. Stop playing this game. It's dangerous. You could really hurt somebody. Especially yourself."

I stare at her, afraid to say anything, afraid to move. Afraid of what might happen if I did.

The look on her face makes me think she can read my thoughts. "I'm sorry," she says. "I've probably said too much. I think I should go."

She heads for the door. I don't try to stop her. With one hand on the handle, she turns to look at me. "I don't think we should see each other for a while."

Something heavy and cold drops into the pit of my stomach. "What?"

"I know we'll see each other at school," she says. "But I need some space. I don't like what I've turned into these last few days. I need time alone. To think."

I want to argue with her, but I'm not sure if I want to beg her to stay or tell her to get the hell out.

"Goodbye, Alden," she says finally.

She hesitates as if she's waiting for me to say goodbye back. But after several seconds, she turns away, and I watch my best friend walk out, the door closing slowly behind her.

TWENTY-TWO

During a dinner of meatloaf and mashed potatoes, another of the meals we eat a lot thanks to my guardian's limited cooking repertoire, Uncle Bill asks me how my day went at school. I guess he hasn't heard yet about the latest "prank" pulled today on the police and on Milton High School's dream couple. But then again, why should he? He's not exactly the hang-out-with-the-other-parents, go-to-PTO-meetings kind of guy. Still, I should tell him. He could find out by reading Milton's local rag and wonder why I didn't mention it.

But what I say is, "Fine."

He doesn't question it. I can see how tired he is. As usual, he ends up in his chair in front of the TV, a beer in hand.

The chair is the only piece of furniture he brought with him when he moved in. When Mom and Dad were alive, there was only the couch. That way we were always sitting together in this room, whether to watch TV or, as we often did, play games. Board games and card games like pinochle and hearts. A lot of the time Charlie was with us, and sometimes so were her mom or dad or both. The games were always fun. What I remember most, though, was the laughter.

I tell my uncle I'm tired, I'm going to bed early, and he wishes me a good night. Once I'm in bed though, I can't sleep. I'm dying to call Charlie, find out what her dad might be saying; see if she learned anything about his conversation with Amy and Greg. But I decide it's best to honor her request for distance. At least until I see her at school tomorrow.

Or maybe I don't call because I don't want to try and guess what it means if she sees my name and number on her phone and doesn't answer.

I'm still awake when my uncle's snoring starts downstairs. I'm still awake when he rouses himself and walks slowly upstairs to his room. And I'm still awake when the snoring starts anew from down the hall.

On nights like this, my mind wanders into the past. I'm back at the annual fair last summer, waiting for Charlie again when I bump into Alan Harder. This time I grab the bag with the gun off the ground before he does, and he runs away, and when I take it to Charlie's dad and explain what happened, he finds the man and arrests him. And no one is shot. Most importantly, my parents are alive.

Or sometimes I picture Dad telling me, "We have some good news to tell you. Something I think you'll really like." And I think of all the possible things he might have been about to say if Alan Harder hadn't stopped him with his gun.

I guess I'll never know.

I once read about a scientific theory that says because human consciousness consists of energy, and since energy never dies, we don't die. That the universe we live in is part of a larger multiverse, and when our physical bodies end, our conscious energy travels to an alternate universe where we get to live our lives again, but this time we make different choices, causing our lives to move in different directions than before.

So I like to think that my parents are now in another universe somewhere, where Alan Harder did not kill them, and an alternate me is with them in an alternate version of our living room, smiling and laughing and playing pinochle.

TWENTY-THREE

I guess Charlie meant it when she said her father wasn't going to drop it.

The school day starts with an unplanned school-wide assembly instead of first period. After we all filter into the auditorium, the principal introduces Charlie's dad, who appears from behind the curtain at the other side of the stage. He looks deadly serious and kind of scary in full uniform as he strides across the stage to the podium. I turn my head to glance at Charlie, who is sitting one row behind me and to my right. A couple of the kids next to her are saying something, but she just nods and looks straight ahead, not returning my look.

"I'm here to talk to you about something very serious," Chief Walker begins. His hands firmly on the podium, he pauses, his steely gaze moving slowly, seeming to take in each and every student in the auditorium. If anyone was still talking they've stopped now. It's pretty clear who Charlie got her intimidating stare from.

Now that he has our attention, the police chief continues. "I'm talking about prank calls," he intones in a deep voice that doesn't need the microphone in front of him to be heard. "In particular, making prank calls to the police, reporting a crime that hasn't happened. Not only is it against the law, it's dangerous. It causes us not only to waste time instead of dealing with real crime, it also causes us to use resources that could be better used elsewhere, in some cases, to save lives. Yet, recently, it seems someone has decided it's fun to make prank calls to the police anyway. And to make it worse, this person, or persons, thinks it's fun to report that a fellow classmate has committed a crime, or even worse, been hurt or killed."

I suddenly feel as if every pair of eyes in the auditorium are on me, and I slump in my seat a little. It's not true, of course. But I still feel like yelling out, *They weren't pranks! Not intentionally!* I bite my lip instead.

Taking in a deep breath so pronounced we can hear it through the podium's microphone, Charlie's dad says, "Well, I'm here to tell you that we are not just laughing this one off. We are taking this very seriously. We are not going to drop this."

I can't help but glance at Charlie again. Again, she does not return it.

"We are conducting a thorough investigation," her dad is saying, "and we will not give up until the culprit or culprits are found. And punished."

This actually causes a few snickers, and a few shushes from teachers, but for the most part, everyone remains quiet and attentive. I do hear one guy in my row whisper to the person next to him, "He's laying it on kind of thick, isn't he?" Maybe he is, but there's no doubt Police Chief Walker is scaring the crap out of me.

He keeps going for a few minutes, finding different ways to say the same thing, before he ends his talk by giving out a special 800 number that has been set up for those with information about the case. These calls will be kept in strictest confidence, he assures everybody. One girl asks if a caller with information has to leave their name, or can they make the call anonymously? The police chief says yes, if you must. Which is kind of ironic when you think about it.

The assembly finally ends, and we all leave the auditorium. I look for Charlie but she seems to have already hurried off to her next class. I do see Greg and Amy walking together. He seems to be trying to comfort her, though he seems more upset than she does.

By the time lunch arrives, everyone is talking about it. Normally, I would sit with Charlie and some of her friends. I passed her in the hall a few times, but she didn't acknowledge me. She did the same in English, the one class we have together. Now, as I stand with my tray, considering whether to go sit with her, she makes my decision for me, glaring at me before turning to say hi to a girl who sits down next to her.

I guess she also meant it when she said she wanted distance from me. I could sit with some guys I know, but I end up eating by myself.

Today's a workout day for Charlie, so it's not out of the ordinary to be walking home without her. I walk part of the way with some friends. Of course, all they want to talk about is the crazy assembly this morning. Who made the prank calls? Was it more than one person? Would the caller do it again? If the caller stopped, how would the police find out who it was? If the caller was caught, how bad would the punishment be? Would it include jail time? How do you think Greg and Amy reacted when Chief Walker pulled them out of class yesterday and told them about the call? On and on. They're so into it, they hardly notice I'm only responding with nods and grunts and one-word answers.

After the two break off in different directions, I continue on alone. I might not normally be walking with Charlie, but I still miss having her next to me right now. Part of me understands why she needs distance. But part of me doesn't. We've been friends for so long surely we can get past this.

The truth is, her need for "distance" hurts. It feels like she's abandoned me. And I never thought she would do that.

It's hard to imagine that last summer, before Alan Harder pulled out his gun, and we'd been happily ragging each other as we always did, I'd been thinking about how Charlie's kiss had felt on my cheek. I'd been considering asking if I could kiss her. What would she have said?

Now that seems a long time ago. And it seems stupid I'd been thinking of her that way.

I'm sure her kiss had meant nothing.

A lot of things changed that awful day. Maybe things changed between Charlie and me as well, and it just took this long for us to realize it.

TWENTY-FOUR

By the time I've reached home, I know what I have to do before anything else: get rid of the bag of "evidence." Charlie would probably freak out if she knew I still had it. With Uncle Bill not coming home till later, I have time.

I pull the bag out from its hiding place in my closet and stare at it for a moment. Then I open it, rummage around, and pull out the backpack. The bloodstain jumps out at me. This time because, again, it's not as much blood as I remember. Which makes me question what it was I'd really seen. Does Greg really have it in him to hit Amy with a backpack full of books? If he was sorry afterward, would Amy really be willing to forgive him for something like that? I know if Amy were my girlfriend, I'd never hit her. Or any girl.

More likely, like Charlie said, Amy really did simply trip and fall, her head first hitting the dugout wall, then landing on the backpack when she hit the ground.

I'm lost in thought, still holding and staring at the backpack, when I hear, "Hey, Alden, you here?"

Crap, it's Uncle Bill! What's he doing home so early? Instead of answering, I drop the backpack into the bag, but it misses and hits the floor.

"Alden, are you upstairs?" I hear him start to move up the stairs. Frantically, I grab for the backpack, but I miss, my fingers only grazing it. My uncle's footsteps are getting louder, closer. I grab for it again, successfully this time, shoving it in the bag then throwing it back into my closet.

Uncle Bill appears at my open doorway. "There you are," he says. "Didn't you hear me calling you?"

I open my mouth. "I...uh..."

"That's okay," he says, wearing a smile on his face I've rarely seen. "I got off early today. Thought you and I could do something. Make up for not getting to share pizza on Sunday. Maybe a movie and then dinner somewhere? If you don't have a lot of homework."

"Actually I do," I say, though, really, all I have are a few easy math problems. "I might need to go to the library..." *Once I figure out how to get the bag I'm hiding out of here without you seeing it.*

"Oh," he says. "Okay. I just thought..."

He looks so crestfallen my heart sinks. "Wait a minute. I don't have to do all of it tonight. I have a few math problems due tomorrow. But the rest can wait."

"You're sure…"

"Yeah," I tell him. "I am."

"Great!" He lights up again, his smile even bigger now. "Let's look at the paper, pick a movie, then do your homework and we'll go."

"I can just check online," I tell him.

"Where can you do that?"

"Here, I'll show you."

I glance back at my closet before leaving my room and following him down the stairs.

TWENTY-FIVE

I actually have a pretty good time. On the way to the movie, Uncle Bill asks me about school, and I surprise myself by telling him more than I usually do. Nothing too deep, mostly what I think about my classes and my teachers, who are my favorites and who aren't. He shares some of what high school was like for him. He was just an average student when it came to English, math, and science, but he did enjoy history, and his best class was shop.

The movie is a dumb comedy, but it's funnier than I expected, and I enjoy myself. I'm most surprised by how much my uncle laughs. He has a booming laugh that rises up from deep in his belly. It's the kind of laugh that's loud, but not annoying because it sounds so pure and heartfelt.

Dinner afterward is at a local diner, and our conversation is mostly about the movie, laughing again as we recap the funniest parts. Uncle Bill even shares how much he loved movies as a kid and when he was younger he went to the movies by himself, sitting through two or three films sometimes. But as he got older and busier, he had to cut back.

That's another surprising thing I've learned: since living with me, I've never seen him sit down to watch an entire movie on television, much less go to a movie theatre.

"You know," I tell him, "anytime you want to go the movies, and I'm busy with homework or school or something, it's okay to go alone."

"Oh, that's okay," he answers. "Even if I wanted to, I don't have the time much with working overtime and all that.

"But," he continues, "maybe you and I could go to a movie every now and then. You could bring your friend Charlie along, if you like. Maybe we could plan to rent a movie to watch together once a week."

"I'd like that."

By the time we pull into our street, the conversation has winded down. He's smiling, but Uncle Bill looks tired—it's past time when he normally falls asleep in his chair. I'm surprised to realize I haven't thought at all about the hidden bag upstairs and the reason it's there. It's been nice not having it dominating my thoughts. But I need to start thinking about how to get rid of it. Tomorrow morning after Uncle Bill has left for work? Or maybe I should do it in the middle of the night.

"You want something to drink, Alden?" my uncle asks. "Why

don't you put something on the TV? I'd like to watch the ten o'clock news before I go to bed."

Normally, he's asleep in his chair before the news, and I'm up in my room. On one of the movie channels, I pick out an action flick I've seen three or four times with Charlie. It's about three-quarters through the movie and will be over by ten.

I expect my uncle to come back with a beer for himself, but he has two ginger ales and hands one to me. He takes the armchair, and I sit on the couch. After a few minutes, he nervously clear his throat. "Alden," he says. "There's something I'd like to talk about."

Uh-oh. He suspects something. He's just been waiting for the right time to bring it up.

"Okay," I say tentatively.

"Today was fun."

When he doesn't say anything more right away, I say, "Yeah, it was." After another moment I add, "Thank you."

"Oh, you don't have to thank me," he says. Then he pauses again. He seems to be thinking, considering what he wants to say, so I wait. Finally, he asks, "Is everything okay?"

Again, my defenses go up. Does he know something and that's why he's asking?

"Sure," I answer, trying to sound casual.

"That's good to hear." He nods his head. More silence. I catch myself fidgeting and tell myself to stop.

"I'm sorry," my uncle says. "I guess you've noticed I'm not much for talking. What's that expression? I'm a man of few words. Your dad came up with that for me."

At the mention of my father, I freeze.

"It comes from living by myself all these years before I moved here," he continues. "I never married, don't have any kids. Never really dated much, to tell you the God's honest truth. You live by yourself long enough, you kind of…lose the ability to have a normal conversation."

I'm thinking: *And you're telling me this, why?*

He looks at me. "If we don't talk much, it's not because of you. I mean it's not your fault or anything. What I'd like is to talk with you more. Hear what's going on in your life besides what your grades are. If that's okay with you."

"Sure," I say, after a moment. "Okay."

He seems relieved, as if he's lifted a big weight off his shoulders. All at once, he says, "You know, you're a lot like your father."

I suddenly feel as if something has sucked all the air out of me.

"I mean, you're a lot like your father when he was your age," he continues. "He was smart, like you are. And curious about a lot of things. He was only a year and a half older than me, but he always seemed older than that. And he was always a lot smarter than me. He enjoyed playing games, all kinds of games, board games, card games, you name it. Of course, you know he loved playing games with you and your mom. After he married your mom, they'd have me over, I didn't live too far away then, and we'd play hearts, pinochle, Trivial Pursuit. I remember when you were a baby, you'd sit in his lap while he was looking at his cards. You were real cute. And you were curious even then, the way you seemed to study his cards, the way you seemed to study everything."

He pauses and looks away for a moment. I can't seem to breathe. Why is he telling me this? Dramatic music is building on the television. The movie's exciting climax is about to happen, but neither of us is paying attention to it. I feel a light panic building inside me, and I have to blink to clear away tears. When Uncle Bill turns back, his eyes are glistening, too.

"When I took a new job that had me on the road a lot, and moved away," he says, "I lost contact with your dad and mom. I don't mean we never talked, but we only talked some on the phone, and even those calls got less and less. I was here for a visit only once after I moved, just for a couple days. You probably don't remember, you were only four or five. I feel awful about missing the funeral, but I didn't know about it because I'd been on the road and no one knew how to get hold of me. I've really regretted…"

He takes in a deep breath. "I've noticed you don't talk much about your father to me, and that's okay. Here I was, somebody you hadn't seen since you were little, and who you probably didn't remember, coming back into your life to try and take over for your dad…and your mom, too. Not that I could ever replace them. I know that. I never wanted to. I just wanted to help."

Another deep breath, then he says, "But I was wondering if you wouldn't mind… If we could talk sometimes…about your father. I could tell you what your dad was like when he was your age. And maybe you could tell me a little of what my brother was like in those years after I moved away and you were growing up. Would that be okay?"

He's looking at me, his eyes pleading, and for a brief moment I'm back on the day of my parents' funeral, standing in the cemetery. The whole town is there, and so many people are crying, including Charlie, who is next to me, holding my hand. But I'm not crying. I'm staring at the two closed caskets and telling myself Dad and Mom are not in there. None of this is real. And, later, when so many people tell me how sorry they are, all I say is "Thank you," over and over. Because to say more means to give in, to admit that what's happening is real.

Charlie is right: I've never talked to anyone about my parents since their deaths. Not even to her, my best friend. Because to do so makes this whole nightmare something I'll never be able to wake up from.

"Sure," I hear myself tell my uncle. Even though I know, down in some deeper part of me, that I can't.

And that, despite all my uncle's done for me, I don't think I'll ever be able to.

TWENTY-SIX

"Well then," my uncle says. "Okay." He glances at the TV and says, "Let's watch the end of this movie, then I'll catch some of the news before I go to bed."

It turns out the movie only has five minutes left, but by the time I click the remote to switch to the news, Uncle Bill is asleep and snoring in the armchair. Normally, I'd head upstairs, but this time I don't, staying on the couch as the news program plays its dramatic theme song. Instead of watching, I sip my ginger ale and stare at my uncle sleeping, wondering how long he's been wanting to talk to me like this, and how I've shut him down every time he mentioned my father.

I'm about to put the remote on the table next to him and go to bed when something in the news broadcast catches my attention.

"...is still missing," the newscaster is saying.

Someone is missing? My eyes on the screen, I sit back down on the couch.

"The Carlson High School junior," the newscaster continues, "was last seen leaving at the end of school last Thursday afternoon."

Thursday. The same afternoon I followed Greg to Miller's Park, where he argued with Amy. A photo of Amy appears on the screen, her bright red hair standing out. She's even wearing the same blue jacket she was wearing that day.

What's going on?

The picture shrinks to the left corner of the screen as a video shows a crying woman standing next to a tearful man who has his arm around her, the woman saying, "If someone knows where our daughter is, I beg you to call us. You don't have to give us your name. We just want our daughter back safe and sound." Below the two people is a caption that reads, "Theresa and James Beaumont, parents of the missing Alycia Beaumont." Now the Carlson police chief is saying something. Then the photo fills up the screen again, the name Alycia Beaumont clearly under it, and I study it closely. The newscaster is speaking again. "She was last seen wearing a white blouse, blue jeans, and the same blue jacket she is seen wearing in this picture."

The girl in the picture isn't Amy, but she looks a lot like her. She has the same bright red hair, a similar complexion. The jacket is even the same shade of blue.

"Again, a special tip line has been set up for anyone with information at 800—"

I don't hear the rest of the number as I tear up the stairs to my room where I yank out the bag from my closet.

On foot, the Carlson and Milton high schools are forty-five minutes to an hour apart. I pull up Google Maps and check Miller's Park in relation to Carlson and Milton. It's what I thought. Miller's Park is halfway between the two high schools. So the walk to the park would be about the same from Carlson High as it had been for me following Greg from Milton.

I pull out the backpack. Could this be Alycia Beaumont's blood, not Amy's? How would I know? Why would Greg have been meeting a girl from another high school? Then I remember something Charlie said. A rumor she'd heard that Greg was cheating on Amy. She'd said there was nothing to it.

Except maybe there was. If Greg had been seeing Alycia behind Amy's back, maybe Alycia had wanted to meet up with Greg to make him choose. Her or Amy? Or maybe she'd told Greg at Miller's Park that if he didn't break up with Amy, Alycia was going to tell her about them. That's why he killed her.

As I think back, I realize there are more differences between the two girls than similarities. Standing next to each other, I'd have no problem telling them apart. But at a distance—the distance from where I'd been hiding to where Greg and the girl had been talking—it would have been very possible to mistake Alycia Beaumont for Amy Sloan.

Maybe Greg killed Alycia. But how do I prove it?

A good investigator takes yet another fresh look at the evidence when needed.

I start with Greg's clothing. All of it is clearly his. Not sure what I'm looking for, I check the pockets of the jeans and jacket. Nothing. Next is the silver cross necklace. Clearly, it's Amy's. It has her name on it. So why did Greg have it? My fingers glide over the broken clasp like I'm trying to read braille. Maybe Greg told Amy he'd get it fixed for her. Then he lost it at the field while killing Alycia and moving her body. Makes sense.

That leaves the backpack. I hoist it up and study it more thoroughly, not that there's much to see. Except for the blood, and maybe a little wear and tear, it looks pretty much the way I remember it from Greg bringing it to school every day. I check the outside pockets again, then run my fingers inside the main part of the bag. Nothing. Frustrated, I yank out my hand.

Something gives, and I freeze. I peer into the backpack and see nothing. Feeling around again, I discover a gap at the very bottom of the backpack. Maybe I accidentally ripped it, but there doesn't seem to be any frayed edges. I work my fingers into the gap as deeply as I can. The gap widens enough for me to get half of my hand in. It's not a rip, it's like somebody cut it to make an extra pocket, then covered it with a fake cardboard bottom. I push further, the hidden pocket widening, my fingers stretching. Finally, it pops open.

Bingo! I pull out a yellowish envelope held closed with a clasp. New evidence? My hands shake a little as I open the clasp and pull up the flap. Reaching in, I pull out a black cell phone. Frowning, I flip it around in my hands. Finding the power button, I push it and the phone turns on. Hmmm. So Greg had what I assume is a second cell. That's not good. It usually means secrets, the kind that always mean trouble. The irony doesn't escape me, Greg and me both using burner phones to hide secrets.

The cell is pretty basic, with no access to the internet or to email. Just calling and texting.

My chest is fluttering as I check the address book. The only phone number listed is for Greg Matthes. So this isn't Greg's phone. It's Alycia Beaumont's. And he was the only one she called on this phone? This is confirmed by the phone log. Each incoming and outgoing call is from or to the same number. I check text messages next. The only thread of messages is labeled Greg. There are a lot of them. Back and forth. Unfortunately, none of them are of the romantic kind. They are mostly messages with times, dates, and abbreviations for what are clearly locations, places for them to meet. Even though these texts were set up to be seen only by each other, they were still being cautious. Or maybe Greg insisted on it because of Amy. I don't know if Alycia Beaumont had a boyfriend *she* was cheating on.

Between sports practices and all the time he spent with Amy, when did Greg have the time to meet up with Alycia for romantic interludes? It looks like they were getting together about once a week. Based on the texts, the week when I was following Greg, if I'd stayed on him one more day, I would've seen something. Come to think of it, how do I know for sure that these meetings were romantic, though what else could they be? There aren't even any heart emojis or anything. I have a sudden thought and quickly scroll to the end of the thread. There it is! Alycia's last text to Greg has them meeting this past Thursday at Miller's Park. After school. Unlike all the other messages, for this one she adds, "I *must* see you."

What about pictures? I click on the photo gallery, and only one picture pops up. It has both Alycia and Greg in a selfie taken by her. Judging by the expression on his face, he wasn't expecting it. Okay, so at least I've got something that definitely shows them together.

There doesn't seem to be anything more to check. Then I notice a stray icon. When I click on it a request for a password pops up. Interesting. I think about it, then type in *Greg*, but it doesn't work. I try *GregandAlycia*. I try abbreviating his name, then abbreviating his and hers together, shortening them each time, mixing in an ampersand. Once I have it down to a simple *G&A*, six pictures pop up.

Whoa.

I click one by one on the first five pictures, and each one shows Alycia and Greg together. The first one shows them kissing. Looks like Alycia used a selfie stick to take the picture. Same with the next few, only with these they had their hands around and all over each other while dressed in only their underwear.

In the sixth and last picture, they're lying in bed. The photo is not completely revealing, but it shows just enough to indicate they're not wearing underwear. They're not wearing anything at all.

I stab the power button, and the cell phone powers off. I slowly put the phone down on a table. From downstairs, I still hear Uncle Bill snoring. He could wake up any minute and drag himself upstairs to his bedroom. Moving quickly, almost frantically, I place the incriminating cell phone back into the backpack that I'm now sure has Alycia Beaumont's blood on it. Then I return the backpack to the larger bag and put the bag back deep into the corner of my closet. No way am I going to get rid of this stuff now. I need time to think.

I should call Charlie. I grab my cell, pull up her name. Then I stop myself. I shouldn't hit her with this new evidence just before she's about to go to sleep. I'll call her tomorrow morning before school.

I hear Uncle Bill moving downstairs, and by the time he's up, I'm in bed, with the lights off, pretending to sleep.

I've got him, I keep telling myself. Greg Matthes killed Alycia Beaumont.

And I can *prove* it!

TWENTY-SEVEN

When all was said and done, no one could figure out why Alan Harder did it. Not the police, not the townspeople of Milton, not the talking heads for the two days it was covered by the cable news networks, not anyone. Harder had no connection with anyone who lived in Milton. And that included my parents.

Once they'd finished their investigation, the best Chief Matt Walker and his police force could determine was that Harder had wandered into Milton on Friday, the day before the fair. This was based on comments by Mr. Strong who said Harder had come into his convenience store late in the afternoon on Friday, bought a coffee and a pack of cigarettes, then left. Security cameras in the store confirmed it. A number of people jumped on the bandwagon, claiming, after the fact, to have seen him earlier on Friday just walking down the street. Two people swore they had seen Harder on that Friday sitting in the park and watching as the fair was being set up. But, ultimately, this could not be confirmed.

Alan Harder was thirty-two the day of the shooting. He didn't have a driver's license, bank account, credit card, or title to a car in his name. His social security number produced an address he hadn't lived at in ten years. They did determine both his parents were dead, and he had no siblings. An aunt was found who lived in a nursing home in a nearby state. But only when she was lucid enough was she able to tell the police that she hadn't seen her nephew in over ten years and knew nothing about his whereabouts since, or why he would do what he did.

Chief Walker still talks about finding out why someday. But Milton seems to have collectively shrugged its shoulders and accepted they'll probably never know the reasons behind why he chose our town and the fair. People shake their heads, wonder what's gone wrong with the world, and then go on with their lives.

Part of me would like to know why he did it. Part of me wonders if knowing would make any difference in my life.

Whether I ever find out or not, my parents are still dead.

TWENTY-EIGHT

Another night of restless sleep has caused me to doubt again. *Should* I call Charlie? She'll probably be pissed, but she'll get over it once I tell her about the cell phone and pictures. Won't she? I have my cell phone in my hand before I decide to wait. She wants space, I'll give her space. She's out of it. I'll do this on my own.

Uncle Bill moves around downstairs. Last night he said he'd be out the door earlier than usual this morning to make up for leaving early yesterday. I consider going downstairs right now to tell him everything, but as I get out of bed, the front door closes, and he's gone.

I haven't opened my investigator's notebook since I got it from behind the shed in the Mattheses' backyard. I should have taken notes last night before bed. I pull it out from its drawer in my desk, sit on the chair, and write. It's all in there. Everything I know.

It makes sense. And yet, as I reread what I've written, I still have doubts about what I should do.

Finally, I pull out the evidence bag from the closet. Open it. Stare inside. I reach in, finding the sandwich bag I've been keeping Amy's silver cross necklace in. Pulling it out, I put it into an outside pocket of my backpack, along with the notebook. I know what Charlie would say about this, but I also know how important this necklace is to Amy. Anonymously or not, I should return it to her. Going downstairs, I eat a couple of Pop-Tarts for breakfast before heading out.

Before going to bed last night, I saw myself walking into the police station this morning, or maybe after school, with the bag of evidence in hand. I'd ask to see Chief Walker, then sit down with him in his office. And like one of those quirky detectives on TV who view evidence and find clues in ways the typical police detective can't, I'd lay it all out for him, telling him what I saw and pulling out each piece of evidence as it became pertinent, all of it pointing to Greg Matthes murdering Alycia Beaumont. He'd been cheating on Amy with her. But she'd wanted more. She wanted him to break up with Amy. She'd met Greg to tell him if he didn't, she'd tell Amy about them. And Alycia had those incriminating pictures. It was enough to make Greg snap.

I'd imagined Charlie being with me. It might make everything I'm saying seem more believable to the police chief if his daughter was there to back me up. But that's not fair to her, I realize now. I'd promised myself I wouldn't implicate her, and I'm going to stick to that.

Besides, I don't know how Chief Walker is going to react when he finds out I'm the "prank caller" he's been looking for. No matter how good my evidence is, he might be furious. Better I be the only one to face any consequences.

Yet the more I think about it, the more I worry about the lack of a body. Clearly, Greg got rid of it—of Alycia, I mean—but, surely, all the evidence, coupled with me telling Chief Walker what I saw, will be enough to make him at least talk to Greg.

But what if Greg stands tough? Greg Matthes is Milton High's golden boy. The pictures and text messages might tarnish his reputation, but for a lot of people, nothing short of a picture or video showing him clubbing his victim to death will be enough to make them believe he could do such a thing. Like Charlie pointed out when we thought it was Amy: Can I say without hesitation that I saw Greg kill her? Maybe a good lawyer could turn the evidence around to make it look like an accident.

She *came after* him, *tripped, hurt herself, got her blood on the backpack, Greg tried to help her. But she ran off. She's missing only because she decided to run away after Greg broke it off with her. Wherever she is, Greg didn't kill her. When he last saw her, Alycia Beaumont was alive.*

Oh, and by the way, about this witness, didn't he first claim it was Amy Sloan he saw killed?

Another horrible image comes to me. The same lawyer talking to the police chief.

How can we trust this Alden Ross when my investigators have turned up evidence showing that this same "witness" is the boy who made two false calls to the police saying he had seen someone hiding a gun, one a father just trying to buy a gift for his child, the other a good student in the middle of school? Clearly, Alden Ross either has a perverse sense of humor or serious mental issues.

That last image makes me shudder, and for a moment, I consider giving up the whole thing. Just getting rid of the evidence and forgetting all about it.

A good investigator never gives up.

How do I make it so the evidence is airtight? What else do I need?

I've made good time. Just a few more blocks to go and school doesn't start for fifteen minutes. As I turn the corner, the Milton High building comes into view, but I also notice a couple walking hand in hand a block in front of me. The girl's long red hair blows in the breeze, and I realize it's Amy and Greg. My first inclination is to find someplace to hide. But I'm not following them this time. I just happened upon them. No need to keep my presence secret. Still, I slow down, giving them a little more distance.

Today, Amy's dressed in a flowery white dress. The color of the flowers matches her hair. She really makes a perfect picture. I can tell she and Greg are talking to each other as they walk, though I can't make out what they're saying. Maybe I'll just cross the street and walk on the other side. I step into the street and start crossing when I notice someone coming out of a side street on the other side a little further up. It's Charlie. Did she see me? She seems to hesitate before turning toward the school. If she did see me, she's ignoring me.

I stop in the middle of the street, not sure which way to go. The beep of a car makes me jump back to the curb. The car drives past me, the driver glaring and calling me a name I can't make out. It's Tommy Zimmerman, the same kid I saw get pulled over by a cop in front of the Matthes house while I was waiting for Charlie to find the backpack.

If I want to be inconspicuous, I'm doing a lousy job of it. I step back onto the curb. Other kids are appearing now, heading toward school. None of them are looking at me. They're each caught up in their own conversations, or are looking at their phones, or moving with dogged determination to get to school.

I take a deep breath, then resume my own walk to the building.

Amy and Greg have stopped and are facing each other. They're not just talking now. What they're doing sure looks like a fight to me.

Instinctively, I jump into a nearby drugstore and grab a couple of things off a shelf, then plant myself at the store window, trying to look like I can't decide which one of these cold medicines I should buy while keeping an eye on the couple.

Most of the other kids slow down to see what's happening. An out-and-out public fight between Milton's royal couple is a big deal.

A sense of déjà vu sweeps through me. I've seen this before. Well, technically, it wasn't Amy Greg was arguing with; it was Alycia. Except I didn't know it was Alycia at the time; I thought it was Amy.

By now, the argument has escalated—on Greg's end at least. He's really going at it, spit flying out of his mouth while he points a finger again and again toward Amy's face. Amy is cowering, saying nothing and looking scared. This is getting serious. Should I do something? I glance at the backpack he's wearing, which he's been using since he bloodied his favorite one. I can't tell how full of books it might be.

All at once, the argument ends, Greg getting in the last word with "I'm sorry about your stupid necklace! Okay? Just…stay away from me! I don't want to see you." And with that, he stalks away from her toward school.

God, did Greg just break up with Amy? The kids who'd slowed their walk to watch now pick up their pace, ready to get the rumor mill going. I notice Charlie walking away, too. Had she stopped to watch the fight?

Amy is all alone. She's just standing there, looking lost, not sure what to do. She might be crying.

Even in sadness, and with the stitches from her forehead cut peeking out from under her hair, Amy is beautiful. Greg may not have killed her, but I know he is capable of killing. All those smiles and pats on the back he gives people, the acts of good sportsmanship he displays on the baseball field; everybody just seems to love him, yet nobody knows the dark side of Mr. Perfect... Except me. I've seen it. And it's bad. If he got mad enough, would he kill Amy, too?

That prospect sends a shudder through me. In a sense, she's also a victim. Or in danger of becoming one. Do I dare tell her just how dangerous he really is? If I could convince Amy her boyfriend's a murderer, I could certainly convince Chief Walker as well.

Amy sits down on a nearby bench, her head down. Turning away from the window, I notice the pharmacist staring at me from the far end of the cold medicine aisle. How long has he been watching me, wondering what I'm doing? Quickly, I put the medicines back on their shelves. After giving a meek wave, I leave.

Amy is still sitting on the bench, her head down. I think she's crying, very softly. Part of me wants to put my arms around her and just hold her. At Miller's Park, Charlie asked me if I had a crush on Amy. Well, maybe. A little. How could anyone not feel sorry for her? How could Greg treat her like this? I stare at her, feeling like a bird is fluttering inside my chest. Taking in a deep breath, I approach her slowly, cautiously. She doesn't seem to notice me.

When I'm only a step or two from her, I ask, "Is there…" My voice sounds like someone rubbed it with sandpaper, and I falter. Amy doesn't lift her head. I clear my throat and try again. "Is there… something wrong, Amy?"

She snaps up. The tears in her eyes make them glisten.

"I'm sorry," I say. "I didn't mean to startle you. You looked… I just wondered if I could help…" God, it's like I've never used words before.

She looks at me, saying nothing.

"I'm Alden. Alden Ross."

"I know who you are," Amy says. "Did you want something?"

"N…no," I stutter. "You just looked like… I just wanted to know if I could…help…"

This is not going well. If the earth suddenly opened up beneath me, I'd gladly let it take me.

"I'm sorry," Amy says, wiping her eyes. "I'm being rude. Thank you for your concern." She stands up. "But I'm fine. I guess I should get going to school. I'm going to be late." She loops her purse over her shoulder. She doesn't have any books or a backpack. But instead of starting to walk, she just stands there, as if she's not sure which direction to go.

Suddenly, in a small voice, she says, "I guess you saw us…fighting. Greg and me."

"Uh, yeah. Sorry," I flounder. "I didn't mean—"

She cuts me off. "I guess everybody else saw, too," she says, looking around. I glance around with her, but anyone who witnessed the fight is long gone, leaving just the two of us.

"It's okay," she says in s shaky voice. "He's just... He didn't mean..." It sounds like she's going to cry again "I really do need to get to school."

I decide to take a chance. "I couldn't help hearing," I say, "something about a necklace?"

She looks at me, her eyes wide. "Well, yes. I...lost it..."

I unzip the outer pocket of my backpack. Holding the plastic sandwich bag like a precious commodity, I carefully pull out the cross necklace.

Amy gives an audible gasp. Her hand goes out, and I place the necklace gently onto her palm.

"Oh my God," she says in awe, turning it over in her hand. "Where did you find it?"

"I was just walking," I fumble, "and I looked down and...there is was."

"I can't believe it. I can't... Thank you." She hugs me, catching me by surprise and knocking me off-balance. She doesn't seem to notice as she says "Thank you" again before releasing me. My face is blazing hot and I know I'm blushing.

"This means so much to me," she says. "This is what we were

arguing about. I'd broken the clasp, and Greg said he'd get it fixed for me. But then he lost it, and I've been upset about it. He said he looked all over for it, he said he'd buy me a new one, but it wouldn't be the same. My parents gave this to me the day I was baptized. He didn't seem to understand that." She shows me the necklace. "Oh, shoot. He didn't get it fixed before he lost it." She lifts the necklace up to her neck and looks at me. "Doesn't it look beautiful?" she asks.

"Uh, yes," I say. I imagine anything would look great hanging from her neck.

"I can't wait to show it to Greg," she says. "I really shouldn't have gotten as mad at him as I did. Him losing it… It was just an accident."

An accident, huh? I want to tell her the truth, but I don't. For now.

"I have got to get to school," she says, putting the necklace in her purse.

"Me too," I say.

She looks at me. Smiles. What a great smile. "Thank you so much, Alden," she says. I don't expect the quick kiss she gives me on the cheek. If she notices me blushing again, she doesn't say anything. Side by side, we walk quickly to school.

I could tell her now, before this gets even more out of hand. Every second I wait is another second Alycia's parents are left without answers, and Amy could be in danger.

Say it! Just tell her!

If I tell her now, though, she'll be horrified. She might not believe me at first. Maybe she'll even think I'm a creep who's obsessed with her and Greg. But at least she'll know. It'll give her time to process. I can offer to show her my evidence later.

But we're in the building now, and Amy is waving to her friends, and the opportunity to confess everything I know is gone.

I watch her as she heads off to her first class, hating myself for being a coward.

TWENTY-NINE

I next see Amy between first and second period, talking to Greg at his locker. She's showing him the necklace. She hands it to him. He studies it briefly as Amy gives him a hopeful smile. Then he gives it back to her. He doesn't seem impressed.

She keeps talking, then tries to take his arm, but he steps back and says something I can't make out. Then, abruptly, he turns and walks away.

Amy is left looking heartbroken. A few kids glance her way but keep going. I want to comfort her, but I worry what people might think. What Amy would think.

Two girls I recognize as friends of hers show up, and soon they've each got an arm around her and are walking with her to her next class. She looks miserable.

"Looks like things aren't all that happy in Amy-Greg land," I hear behind me. I recognize the voice, of course, and turn to face Charlie. Her arms are crossed. "Any idea what that's about?" she asks.

"Uh, no," I say.

"Are you sure?" she says, eyes squinting. "Looks to me like she has her necklace back."

When I don't say anything, she adds, "That argument I saw them having on the way to school sounded like it was about a necklace. *The* necklace."

So she *had* watched the argument. "I wouldn't know."

"Oh, really? That wasn't you I saw sneaking into the drugstore to watch from the window?"

I don't say anything. Charlie beckons me to follow her to the far wall, which I do, reluctantly, out of the way of student traffic.

"Alden, tell me you didn't give the necklace back to her yourself. Tell me that's not the reason the two of you were seen walking into school together. Tell me you slipped it into her locker or her purse without her knowing it."

I don't say anything, but the answer must be clear on my face because she rolls her eyes and says, "Alden…"

"What do you care?" I can't keep the defensiveness from my voice.

"You don't want anything that might connect you to Amy or the phone calls."

"Don't worry, I won't mention you if your dad questions me."

"I'm worried about *you*."

"Well, you don't have to be."

"You should have gotten rid of the necklace with the rest of the evidence."

When I don't say anything, her glare intensifies, and she seems to rise to her full six-foot height as she bears down on me. "You did get rid of the rest of the evidence, didn't you?"

Now would be the time to tell her what I've learned since we last talked. But why should I? Best friends stick together, and when things got really tough, Charlie didn't stand by me. She walked away. "I thought you wanted to keep your distance from me," I blurt out.

Her eyes narrow even more. In the past, I wouldn't have said anything.

Not this time.

"You don't want to hang with me anymore, then don't," I tell her, my tone sounding different even to me.

"Alden…" she tries.

"Just leave me alone!" I hiss.

And then it comes tumbling out of me before I can stop it. "I don't need you watching over me. Feeling sorry for me all the time because of what happened to my mom and dad. I don't need it anymore. I don't want it!"

As long as we've been friends, I've never seen such a look of deep hurt on Charlie's face as I do now. I start to take back what I said—I want to—but for some reason I don't. Something stops me.

And then it's too late. Charlie's expression changes from hurt to anger.

For a moment, I'm afraid of what she might do to me. Maybe she is, too, because all at once she turns and, without a word, marches off.

The feeling of something dark and heavy in my stomach keeps me in place. When the next bell finally rings, I manage to move, getting to my next class a couple of minutes late.

Along the way, I can't help feeling like I've just broken something I'll never be able to fix.

THIRTY

By the end of the school day, I've seen Amy three more times: twice walking in the hall and once at lunch. Each time, Greg is not with her. It's most notable in the cafeteria, where she sits with a group of friends. At one point, Greg comes in, but instead of going to Amy, he hooks up with a group of guys from the baseball team, and they leave the room. I notice Amy staring sadly at him, but he never looks at her. After he leaves, she tries joining her friends in conversation, but with difficulty.

I look for Charlie, but she never makes an appearance.

At the end of the day, I decide to use a different exit, taking a way home that's not used as much by students. I told myself I wasn't in the mood to be near anybody, but once I'm out of the building I'm wondering what Amy might be doing. Normally, she'd be in the stands watching Greg at baseball practice. But after today, maybe she, too, is walking home alone.

Pivoting hard, I decide to look for her, and I almost crash into somebody. "Whoa, slugger, watch out there." Big hands grab my shoulders.

"Sorry," I say automatically as I look up.

"No problem," Greg Matthes says. "How are you doing?" he asks.

I'm sure there have been a few times in my life at Milton High when Greg has given me a friendly hello or even a pat on the back—he seems to do that with everyone—but at the moment, I can't think of any time before now. His smile is full of welcome and encouragement. His hands still grasp my shoulders.

"I'm…fine." My voice sounds like it's coming from somewhere far away.

"That's good." Thankfully, he releases his hold.

"Don't…don't you have baseball practice?" I hear myself ask. "Don't the playoffs start next week?"

"I've got a few minutes," he responds. "I wanted to talk to you, actually. I wanted to thank you for finding Amy's necklace and giving it back to her."

"You're…welcome," I manage. My mouth is suddenly dry, and I try to swallow.

"Amy loves that necklace," Greg continues. "Dumb me, I was supposed to get it fixed for her, but I lost it. One minute, it's in my pocket, the next, it's gone. I looked all over for that thing. I'm really glad you found it."

"Sure," I say, getting at least some of my voice back. "No problem. Listen, I need to get going—"

"Where did you find it?"

A light pounding begins in my chest. "Pardon?" I say.

"Where did you find it?" Greg asks again. "Do you remember? Amy told me you were just walking somewhere, looked down, and there it was. Do you remember where?"

"No, I...I don't." I glance right and left to see if anybody is walking by.

Greg shrugs. "I was just curious." He takes a step as if to leave, then stops and turns back. "Actually, the last time I remember having the necklace was last Thursday. I was walking on Bronco Street—you know where that is, don't you? I was actually on my way to get it fixed. I was almost there, but when I reached in my pocket, I realized it was gone. I felt awful." He shakes his head. "Is that where you found it?"

"Huh?"

"Bronco Street. Is that where you found it?"

"Uh, yeah," I tell him. "Come to think of it, that is where I found it. On Bronco."

"Really?"

"Yeah."

"Well, thanks again, man." He gives a wave and turns. Happy to get away from him, I leave in the opposite direction. Suddenly I feel his hand on my shoulder again. "Wait a minute," I hear. "Stupid me."

He pulls on my shoulder, turning me around. "It wasn't Bronco."

"What?" I say.

"It wasn't Bronco," he repeats.

His smile is still the same, but his eyes have changed. They've grown darker, more intense. "What was I thinking? I was walking on Turner Street when I realized I'd lost it. That's way across town from Bronco. In fact, I was nowhere near Bronco that day." He moves toward me a step. "How the heck did her necklace end up all the way on Bronco?"

The thudding in my heart has reached my head, pounding. I want to rub my forehead, but I keep my hand still. "I don't know," I say in a shaky voice. I try to laugh, but it comes out strangled. "I really don't remember where I found it."

"But you did," Greg says, his smile growing thinner. "Find it, I mean. So I was thinking you might've found something else I've been missing. Something really important to me. I know it sounds silly, but it has all these patches on it that I've put on over the years. They have sentimental value for me, I guess. You know what I'm talking about, right? Why getting it back to me is so important? Why I'd do just about anything to get it back?"

He moves closer. "Anything."

He says this last with a chuckle even though his smile is barely showing now. He seems to be waiting for me to say something.

"Uh" is all I manage at first. I clear my throat and try again. "Uh, sure," I say. "I can understand that."

"Last time I remember having it," he goes on, "I was home. Alone. I had it. In my hands. Then I put it back. I swear I did." His voice is changing. The smile disappearing. "The next day, I went to get it and it wasn't there." He comes even closer. "Do you know where it could be, Alden?"

I open my mouth, but nothing comes out. At six feet two, he towers over me. "I asked you a question," he says. "Or maybe I could ask Charlie. She might know… Right? Oh, and by the way, I found something interesting. In my backyard, of all places. Behind the shed. It made for an interesting read. I left it where I'd found it, though. In case the person who lost it came back for it. Because I know how bad it feels to lose something important. And you know what? He came back. So it's all good. Except, now I want back what belongs to me. Do you know what I mean?"

He's standing so close it feels like he might topple over me. Crush me under his weight. My throat feels clogged. I know if I try to talk, to breathe, I'll start choking. He's staring at me, and now that he's dropped the smile, I can see the creature behind it, like the removal of a mask. A creature capable of striking out, suddenly and without warning, with whatever weapon available.

"Alden," he says, "where is my—"

"Hey, Greg, there you are." The unexpected interruption comes from one of his teammates coming toward us, wearing a baseball team practice shirt. I can't remember his name. "Coach has been wondering where you are. Practice started."

Greg steps back but doesn't look away as he says, "I'll be there in a minute."

"I think you need to come now. He's pissed. You know how he gets close to playoffs."

Irritation flashes across Greg's face as he shouts back over his shoulder, "All right. I'm coming!"

I should take advantage of the moment and get out of here. Fast. But my legs feel heavy. I can't get them moving. Greg seems uncertain now. Then, the smile returns, but it's sad this time as he leans in and says, "You know, Alden, I don't think I ever really told you how sorry I was about what happened to your parents. It was awful. You have just your uncle now, right? No other family? I bet you're glad he's here to take care of you. Otherwise, what would you do if something happened…?"

Letting his voice trail off, his smile changes again. "Gotta go," he says, waving as he retreats, the mask solidly in place, exuding nothing but charm and affability. "We'll talk again soon."

He pauses for emphasis. "I promise." He joins his teammate and, together, they walk away.

Everything inside me is swirling, pulling, as if I'm trapped in a whirlpool. If I try to move, I'll collapse.

But I have to move.

Eventually, I start walking, desperately trying to figure out what I'm going to do next.

THIRTY-ONE

It takes me a while to gather my panicked thoughts together. When I'm finally able to think again, one thing pops out.

He *knows*. Greg Matthes *knows*.

Okay. What exactly does he know?

He doesn't know I have the bag of bloody clothes he tried to get rid of.

He did find my notebook. And he read it. And he may have been babysitting his sister, but he was watching when I came back to get it and found out it was mine. What I'd written in my notebook at that point told him I had the necklace, but he didn't know the backpack was missing until the next day when he'd finally decided to get rid of it.

You know what I'm talking about, right? Why getting it back to me is so important?

He put two and two together and realized I had the bag.

Why I'd do just about anything to get it back.

And if he knows I have his backpack, he might have assumed I found the cell phone hidden inside, with the pictures and the texts on it.

Anything.

I'm such an idiot!

Why I'd do just about anything to get it back.

He's going to come after me. He's already killed one person. What's one more?

Or maybe I could ask Charlie…

Or two more.

You have just your uncle now, right? No other family?

Or three? Would Greg really kill the two people I love the most?

Anything.

What do I do next? Should I warn them? What if I just give everything back to Greg? His bloody clothes. His backpack. I can pretend I didn't find the cell phone. And I'll promise not to tell anybody.

Ever.

Yeah, he'll believe that.

And what about Amy? What's to stop him in the future from killing her if she does something he doesn't like? Or says something? I need to tell her. For her own safety. The sooner the better.

I have to talk to Chief Walker. It's not just about me anymore. Or solving what happened to Alycia Beaumont. It's also about protecting Charlie and my uncle. And Amy. I can't do that alone. Whatever the consequences are for not telling him before, I'll face them.

With my decision made, I actually feel a little better. As if it's a sign, Amy appears just a couple of blocks ahead of me. I guess I'd been so lost in thought, I hadn't even noticed her.

She's walking with her head down, her shoulders slumped. She has plenty of friends she could be walking with, if she wanted. Maybe she wants to be alone.

I run to catch up, and she must hear me coming but she doesn't turn around, so I try clearing my throat. Nothing. I clear my throat again, then try, "Uh, Amy?"

Abruptly, she stops and turns, a startled look on her face. I skid to a stop to keep from bumping into her.

"Oh, it's you, Alden," she says, letting out a sigh. "You surprised me."

"Sorry, I didn't mean to," I say.

"It's okay." She gives me a smile, but it looks sad.

"Is it okay if I walk with you?" I ask.

She hesitates, then says, "Okay. If you want to."

I fall into step with her, and we walk in silence. I try to think of ways to tell her her boyfriend is a killer. None of the ways I come up with seem right—not that any way is going to feel "right." Suddenly telling her doesn't seem like a great idea. Maybe when she breaks off toward her house, I'll just walk home, grab the evidence bag, and go straight to the police station. Let Chief Walker be the one to tell her.

Amy says something I don't catch.

"I'm sorry," I say, "I didn't hear…"

"I wanted to thank you again," she says. "For finding my necklace. I was convinced I wasn't ever going to see it again."

"Well then, I'm glad I did."

Her smile can't disguise the sadness in her eyes.

"I guess Greg was relieved." Oh God. What a dumb thing to say. Especially since I know the answer.

She hesitates. "Yes," she says. Suddenly, she's crying. She tries to hide it by turning her head.

"I'm sorry," I say again. "I didn't mean—"

"It's not your fault. You didn't do anything. I'm just…" Again, she hesitates. "I just haven't had a very good day. I guess sometimes God gives us challenges."

I'm not sure how to respond. We start walking again, but after a minute, Amy stops again. Fresh tears stain her face. I take a chance. "Do you want to talk about it?"

She looks at me.

"I mean, if you want to, I'll listen," I add.

"You're sweet," she says after a minute. "But I…"

She falters yet again. "Oh, who am I kidding?" she says. "It's not as if everybody doesn't already know. Saw or heard about us fighting. My friends all say they want to help, but it feels like they're crowding me. They're more interested in just telling me what to do. Maybe talking to someone different will help."

She sounds more like she's talking to herself. I wait as she wipes her face and takes a breath. "Let's keep walking," she says. We start moving again and haven't gone a block when she says, "Greg and I are…having problems. I'm afraid he might want to break up with me. And I don't know why. Or what it is I've done." Saying this causes her to choke up. She clears her throat. "Why do guys do stuff like that?"

How would I know? I've never even had a girlfriend.

As if she knows this already, she doesn't wait for me to respond. "I've noticed there's been something wrong," she continues. "He's been so distant. I've asked him if he was all right, but he just says he's fine. He's not though. Maybe he's wanted to break up with me for a long time and doesn't know how to tell me."

Before I can think of anything helpful, Amy continues. "Since I got home from church camp, he's been getting angry. Especially after the police talked to us about that prank phone call. Why would somebody do something like that? Usually, Greg's so nice to everyone and so kind to me. But not the last couple of days. He doesn't seem to understand why I was so upset about the necklace. How much it means to me. He said I was overreacting. But when I told him you'd found it, when I showed it to him, I thought he'd be happy for me. But he's just as angry. Maybe more so. I don't know what I've done. Or what I can do to make him happy again. Something's bothering him, but I can't help him if he won't tell me what it is…"

Her voice trails off. I feel awful for her. I want to help her feel better, though I know what I have to tell her will only make her feel worse. Still, before I go to Chief Walker, for her protection, she needs to know.

She wipes her eyes, then looks at me. "I'm sorry," she says. "You don't even really know me. I shouldn't assume you want to hear all this."

"It's okay."

"No, it's my problem. I should just talk to Greg. Get the truth from him. Whatever it is."

She straightens up, wipes her face one more time. "I should go home now. Thank you for listening to me, Ald—"

"I think I know what's bothering him," I blurt out.

Her eyes open wide in surprise. "Why would you know?"

I start with the least alarming offense. "Greg's been cheating on you."

She looks stunned. Any minute now, I expect her to start shouting that I don't know what I'm talking about, I don't know Greg, he would never do that to her.

But she doesn't. Instead, after a long moment, she breaks her stare and turns away. "I think I've known for a while now that there was someone else. I kept telling myself I was wrong, that I was imagining it."

Her voice seems hollow, her body half-turned from me as she stares at nothing in particular. It looks like she might start crying again, but she doesn't.

I can't just leave it at that; I have to tell her all of it. "Amy," I start, but she suddenly turns back.

"How do you know?" she asks. "Did you see them together somewhere, holding hands, kissing? Do you know who it is? Is it someone who goes to Milton?"

I take a breath. Speak carefully. "No, she doesn't go to Milton. Her name is…was…Alycia Beaumont."

"I don't know her," Amy says after thinking about it. "But the name seems familiar… Do you know how long he's been seeing her?"

"No, I don't."

"Did you see them together?" she repeats. "Wait a minute. You said 'was.' Did they break up?" This last part she said with hope in her voice.

"No," I say slowly. "Something bad happened. Something—"

She cuts me off. "What are you talking about?" Instead of expecting a response, she changes gear. "Wait a minute. Why is that name familiar? Why—"

All at once, she stops. I study her face as her expression changes, a look of horror dawning on her face, her eyes widening in realization. "I heard it on the news. And I saw it on a poster somewhere. Alycia Beaumont. That girl from Carlson. She's missing. But what does that have to do with Greg?"

She faces me, hands on hips. She knows what I'm about to say. I can see it in her face. Because, maybe, the new angry Greg has made her see something in her boyfriend she's never seen before. Something that scares her, that might make her believe he could hurt somebody.

How did I get myself into this situation? What made me think I should be the one to tell her this?

A good investigator knows when to make the tough choices.

"She isn't just missing." My throat is so dry I don't sound like me. "She's dead. Greg killed her."

"Greg killed…" She stares at me. "No." Her voice rises. "Greg would *never* do something like that. Why would you say that?"

"I'm sorry," I say.

She starts backing away. "This is…cruel. I'm leaving. I've got to get home." She turns, takes a couple steps, then suddenly turns back to me. "How do you… No! Don't. Just stay away from—"

"I saw him do it."

There. Now it's out. I wait to see how she'll react.

A good investigator knows when to face the consequences of his tough choices.

"You're lying," Amy says after a moment. "Where did you see him?"

"Miller's Park," I tell her.

"Miller's Park?" she echoes back in disbelief. "What was Greg doing way out there? How did you see him?"

Do I tell her I was following Greg? What reason would I give her?

"I was just…walking by."

A good investigator knows when to fudge the truth.

"Are you sure it was Greg?"

"Yes. I thought the girl was you. Alycia Beaumont looked a lot like you, especially from a distance. She had the same red hair as you do. She was even wearing a blue jacket like the one you wear sometimes."

A new realization crosses her features. "You're the one who made that call about me and Greg. The cops said it was a prank."

"It wasn't meant to be. I really thought he'd killed you." The emotion in my voice surprises me.

"But it was really this Alycia Beaumont you saw him kill?"

"Yes."

"You were wrong about her—you could be wrong about him."

"I'm not."

Amy shakes her head. "Greg's being angry doesn't mean—"

"I have proof," I interrupt.

"What kind of proof?" She looks at me as if I'm lying.

My back straightens. "I can show you."

"Where is it?"

"It's at my house."

"Your house?" Amy sounds suddenly wary.

"Yes," I say. "I've got it hidden there."

"You live with your uncle, right?"

I nod.

"Will he be there?"

"No. He's still at work. I don't expect him home till later."

"Is this some kind of cheap trick to get me alone with you in your house—"

"No! God, no, I'd never do something like that!" I'm horrified she would think that. "I just want to show you what I have."

She studies me. "That's all? Do you promise?"

"I promise." I hold up my hand.

"Okay. Let's go." She says this last with a tremble in her voice. She doesn't want to look at it anymore than I want to show it to her. But she needs to hear the truth so she knows Greg for what he really is.

My heart pounding, I lead the way to my house.

THIRTY-TWO

Just like I told her, Uncle Bill is not home. Once inside, I notice her glancing around, checking things out. "Do you want something to drink?" I ask her.

"No, thank you," she says. "Where's your proof?"

"I've got it hidden upstairs in my room."

"Your bedroom?" Amy sounds more wary. "Can't you bring it downstairs?"

"I don't want my uncle to see it if he suddenly comes home."

"I thought you weren't expecting him till later."

"I'm not. But I can't be totally sure."

She glances around the house again.

"I guess I could bring it down," I say, heading toward the stairs.

"No, that's all right," she says abruptly.

Amy follows me upstairs to the second floor, and we head down the hall to my room. She keeps looking left and right, as if she expects someone to jump out at any moment. When we reach my room she waits for me to go in first, then, moving cautiously, she follows me in. As she looks around I feel embarrassed at how barren my room looks. Most teenagers would have posters on the walls, pictures on desks and tables, something. Except for the single photo of my parents, I have nothing. It looks more like a prison cell than a bedroom.

"I've got it over here." I head into the closet and come out with the bag. Without thinking about it, I sit on my bed. Amy hesitates, then pulls out my desk chair and sits on it, keeping a fair distance between us.

Before opening the bag, I tell her, "I'm sorry about this. I really am."

"Just show me what you have," she says, looking grim and a little scared.

I take a deep breath. "When I realized Greg had killed you...I mean her...I panicked. I ran home." No need to tell her Charlie had any part in this. "I called the police, anonymously. I used a pay phone. I didn't mention you or Greg then, just that a girl had been killed. But the police didn't find anything. Not a body, no sign of an attack, nothing. The next day, I went back and looked around. That's when I found your necklace. At the time I thought it confirmed it was you he killed, but now I know Greg had it. It must have fallen out of his pocket while he was killing her or maybe when he was getting rid of her body."

Amy cringes at that.

After a few seconds, I continue. "I think he hit her with his backpack. It was filled with books, and he swung it at her."

"You *think*?" Amy says.

"They were standing behind the dugout wall on one of the fields. I didn't actually see him do it, but I heard Alycia cry out, then saw the backpack for a second, up above the wall then down, like he was swinging it. I heard the backpack hit her."

"If you didn't see all of it, how can you be sure?"

Without saying a word, I reach into the bag and pull out the backpack. She stares at it for a moment. With all the familiar sports patches on it, she knows that it belongs to Greg. "Is that blood?" she says in a timid voice.

"Yes. I found blood on the dugout wall. I think the force of the bag of books hitting her caused her to hit her head against the wall before she fell. Some of the blood must have splashed on Greg's backpack. Or maybe Greg dropped the backpack after he hit her and her head landed on it when she fell, and that's how the blood got on it."

"He told me he'd torn the strap, which is why he hasn't been using it the last few days," she says in a distant voice.

"I walked around the edge of the wall," I continue in as gentle a voice as I can, "and saw him holding it. Alycia was lying on the ground at his feet."

"How…how did you get the backpack?"

I hesitate. "He was hiding it in his room."

She looks at me. "You broke into his house?"

"Yes."

I expect her to be upset about that, but she says nothing. Continuing, I reach into the bag again and pull out the smaller bag containing Greg's bloody clothes. I take them out one by one and show each item to Amy. She gives a little gasp when she sees the shoes, which I show her last. Perhaps she recognizes them in particular, making it impossible for her to deny that the clothes, just like the backpack, belongs to her boyfriend.

"Did you break into his house to get those, too?" she asks.

"He tried to throw them away. I got them out of the trash can before garbage pickup the next day."

She seems resigned to what I'm telling her. "You've been spying on him, haven't you? For how long?"

"Since Saturday, the day after he killed Alycia."

"Not before?" She stares at me.

I stare back.

"You *were* spying on him before Saturday," Amy says. "You followed him. That's how you saw him…hurt that girl. Right?" She takes my silence for a yes. "That's kind of weird, you know. But I've heard that about you."

"What?" My face is suddenly hot. "How did…"

"Rick Kellerman thought he noticed you spying on him, I heard. He's pretty upset. "

Suddenly, everything feels twisted. It looks like I'm not as good at this as I thought. If Rick Kellerman noticed, how many others have?

"Hey, don't worry," Amy says. "There are people who think I'm weird because I'm a Christian and I'm not afraid to say so. I won't judge you for it. I know what happened to your parents." She leans toward me. "I understand. I do. You're trying to help people. You don't want what happened to you to happen to anyone else. If you hadn't spied on Greg, I wouldn't know what he'd done. Who knows, he might've attacked *me* someday."

I stare at her, awestruck. Amy really does seem to understand; she even appreciates it. She understands more than Charlie, my supposed best friend, who keeps telling me I should stop. Charlie, who, when I need her the most, isn't here for me.

"Are you okay?" Amy asks.

"Uh…yeah. Thank you for that."

She gives me the briefest of smiles, then turns serious again. "Is there anything more you have?" she asks. "You haven't shown me anything that proves absolutely Greg and this Alycia were seeing each other." Her voice becomes shaky. "Did you see them kissing before Greg killed her?"

"No. She kept trying to hug him, but he'd push her away. Then they were arguing."

"Then maybe he wasn't seeing her. Maybe it was something entirely different. Maybe he didn't—"

"There is one more thing," I say.

"What?"

Reaching into the backpack, I pull out the cell phone. Hoping there was enough power left after I'd turned it off before, I turn it on. After a split-second hesitation, the screen lights up. "He had this hidden in here. I found it by accident. It belonged to Alycia." After the phone finishes powering up, I extend it to her. "I'm so sorry."

At first, Amy does nothing. Then, slowly, as if I'm giving her a bomb that might explode at any moment, she takes it from my hand. "Go to the text screen," I tell her. "You'll see texts between them. They're all places where they met. About once a week, it looks like. The last one shows they were meeting at Miller's Park. The text date is the date she was killed."

"Okay. So he was meeting her. That still doesn't mean they were—"

"There's a picture." I don't like telling her about it and wish there was some way I could do this without her seeing it, but she needs to know the truth. She deserves to know.

"Check gallery," I tell her.

Amy touches the icon and brings up the only picture there. The selfie of Alycia and Greg together, Greg looking like he hadn't expected the picture to be taken.

Amy's face falls . "I guess this proves it." She seems to be fighting tears. "Is that everything?"

She doesn't need to see any more. I don't want her to be hurt any more than she is. "Yes," I answer, maybe a little too quickly. I stick my hand out for the phone, but she ignores me.

"Was there anything else on this thing?" she asks without looking up.

"No, nothing," I say. "I'll take that." I fight to keep a sudden urgency out of my voice.

"What's this other icon? It needs a password."

"It's nothing. There's nothing there."

She looks up and frowns at me. "Why are you acting funny?"

"I'm not," I say with a shaky laugh, which only makes things worse.

She stares at me. Her sudden look of determination reminds me of Charlie. "What's the password, Alden?" she asks.

"Amy," I plead, "you don't want to—"

"What's the *password*?" she snaps.

I hesitate, then before she snaps at me again, "G and A."

"For Greg and Alycia," she mutters under her breath.

"The ampersand for 'and.' No spaces," I add feebly as she punches in the correct letters.

A sudden gasp tells me she has accessed the hidden pictures. I wait as she swipes her thumb across the phone. The look of horror on her face grows as the photos make it very clear that Greg's relationship with Alycia went far beyond kissing. Once she has seen them all, she closes her eyes for a moment, then extends her hand with the phone and says, "Take this. Please take this."

Like it's hot to the touch, I take it, shut it off, and toss it into the backpack. Just as quickly, I put all the evidence back into the bag while Amy sits very still. Then I return to the bed and sit down. And wait.

Her look of horror has changed to sadness. I'm not sure if it's a question or a statement when she says, "You're taking that to the police."

I answer anyway. "Yes. I think it would mean more if you came with me."

"When?"

"As soon as possible. Maybe right now."

"We should find Greg. Show him what we have. Confront him."

"What? No!" I say. "He *killed* Alycia! And he threatened me."

She looks at me, eyes widening. "He threatened you?"

"In so many words. He knows I have the backpack and the phone."

"How did he find out?" Before I can answer, she waves her hand. "Never mind."

"I'm sorry," I tell her, though I'm not sure why I'm apologizing.

"Don't be," she says. "It's not your fault."

Her emotions have veered all over the place. Now she's back to angry.

"If you don't want to go with me—" I start.

"I'll go," she says suddenly.

"Really?" I ask, surprised.

"Like you said, it'll mean more if I'm with you."

She surprises me again by sitting next to me on the bed. Her sudden closeness makes me nervous, but she doesn't seem to notice. "Look, I want to help," she says in a quieter voice. I'm suddenly warm all over. Our legs brush, sending a shudder through me. "You've done so much work. I want to show you how grateful I am."

She can't possibly mean what I think she means. This is Amy Sloan, for God's sake. Sweet, innocent, cross-wearing Amy Sloan. To confirm it, she adds, "So I'll go with you," and I exhale a little shakily. "We'll show the evidence to the police chief together tomorrow."

"Tomorrow?" My throat is rough and dry and my voice raspy.

"If we go now, I don't know if I can… I'm still having trouble believing that Greg…" She takes a deep breath to settle herself. "As horrible as it sounds, what you've told me helps explain why he's been so different lately. I need time to process this. There's no school tomorrow because of the teachers' workshop. Let's take it to the police first thing in the morning. And I'll back up everything you say. Here, I'll give you my phone number, just in case. You want to give me yours?"

Everything seems to be happening so fast all of a sudden, and somehow too slow at the same time. But, of course, she's right. One more night's not going to make a difference. The important thing for now is she knows the truth about Greg, and she'll stay away from him. "Sure," I say.

We exchange numbers. "I'll meet you at the police station at 9:00 a.m." She gives me a soft, uncertain smile.

"Okay."

"Is that bag going to be okay here?"

"I've had it all this time," I say. "It's safe here. It's just my uncle and me, and he's hardly ever in my room."

"Okay," she says. "I have a younger sister and brother. They're always snooping. If I hid it at my house, they'd find it."

I nod. "Tomorrow then."

"9:00 a.m.," she repeats, then points at me. "Don't forget."

Like I could. "I won't."

We stare at each other. I guess it's time to say goodbye. "Let me put this away," I say, indicating the bag. When I come back out of the closet, there's Amy. "Thank you, Alden," she says. "You might have saved my life." With that, she hugs me.

It catches me by surprise, and I'm clumsy and awkward as I hug her back, but we remain this way for a second or two. When she pulls away, I notice again how perfectly her bright red hair frames her face, making her blue eyes sparkle.

The distinct sound of someone clearing his throat jolts us apart. Uncle Bill stands in the doorway. "Um, I just wanted to tell you I'm home." He looks about as uncomfortable as I feel. "I can just—"

"I need to go home anyway," Amy says.

My uncle is giving me a look, and I find my voice. "Amy, this is my uncle Bill. Bill Ross."

"Very nice to meet you, sir," Amy says in a sweet voice, any sign of how our previous conversation affected her gone from her face. "Your nephew was helping me with some of my homework."

"You don't have to go on my account," Uncle Bill says.

"My mom'll be expecting me." She looks at me and smiles. "Bye, Alden."

"Bye," I say back.

Uncle Bill moves aside to let her pass. She steps into the hall, and as soon as my uncle turns his head away from her, she mouths to me, "See you tomorrow."

I give her a barely perceptible nod, and she walks away, down the hall.

As soon as we hear the front door close, Uncle Bill, seemingly flustered, says, "I'm sorry if I interrupted something. I didn't mean for her to leave."

"It's all right," I say. "She really did have to go."

"Is she someone, you know, special? A girlfriend?"

"No," I tell him, but he doesn't seem to hear me.

"'Cause, if you ever need to talk about stuff like that, you know…"

"She's just a friend," I tell him, wishing he'd get off the subject. "I was helping her with math."

"Uh-huh." He doesn't seem to believe me. "Anyway, I got off early again today. I'm off tomorrow and you don't have school, so I thought we could do something."

"You mean tomorrow?"

"Well, I was thinking tonight. See a movie. Maybe even two. Unless you have other plans?" He raises his eyebrows, tilting his head in the direction of the front door.

"No, I don't have any plans," I say quickly.

"Movie it is then," he says, his face beaming. "We'll see one, then we'll decide what to do. If we want to do another, we'll just have candy and popcorn for dinner."

He looks so happy I don't have the heart to say no. "Sure," I say.

He slaps me on the back and, with my insides still churning from my conversation with Amy, I get my phone to check movie times.

THIRTY-THREE

I thought seeing a movie with Uncle Bill would allow myself to concentrate on something, but it doesn't. My head is filled with scenarios of how tomorrow's meeting with Chief Walker might play out, the best one ending with Chief Walker praising me for a job well done, and even suggesting I might make a good police investigator someday. The not-too-bad one has him yelling at me for taking the law into my own hands instead of coming to him sooner. The worst scenario ends with Chief Walker telling me, "Sorry, son, you broke too many laws getting this evidence, we can't use it. I'm afraid I have to put you in jail."

After the first movie is over, about which I remember virtually nothing, it's clear Uncle Bill is having a great time and wants to grab candy and popcorn and stay for another movie. I give in and say yes, even though I feel dead on my feet. Even if we did go home though, I doubt I could sleep.

We're about halfway through the second movie when a new, horrible thought strikes me. What if Greg is trying to break into our house while we're here? After all, he thinks I broke into his, even if it was really Charlie. Maybe he'd try the same thing to get his stuff back. He might have been watching my house, just like I watched his, and saw Uncle Bill and I leave.

Oh God. I have to get out of here. I glance at my uncle; he's not going to want to leave unless he's given a damn good reason.

A good investigator knows when to improvise.

"Uncle Bill," I say in as weak a voice as possible, "I don't feel good."

My uncle half turns to me, trying to keep his eyes on the screen at the same time. "What did you say?"

"I don't feel good," I say again, as if I'm on death's door. "I think I might be sick." The gagging noise I make sounds almost real.

Quickly, he straightens up, looks around on the floor, and comes up with one of our empty popcorn containers. "Here, do you need…"

"No, I don't think… I just feel sick all of a sudden. Can we go home?"

"Sure, sure," Uncle Bill says, glancing at the screen once more, but then helping me to stand.

We make our way out of the theater, a few people glaring at us as we pass them. Once we're in the lobby, Uncle Bill fusses over me. "Are you sure you can wait till we get home? You could…" He points toward the men's room.

"No, that's okay."

"Maybe I should take you to the emergency room—"

"No!" My voice is too loud, too strong. I return to being weak and sickly. "It's probably because of all the popcorn and candy I ate," I say, even though I didn't really eat that much. "I just want to go home and rest."

"Sure, sure. Let's go."

Uncle Bill ushers me quickly out of the lobby and into his truck. He breaks a few speeding laws to get me home. Once there, I worry that Greg is in the house, that we're about to catch him in the act. But he's not. Uncle Bill finds a half-filled bottle of Pepto-Bismol bought by my parents a good year before they died. It's well past its expiration date, but he makes me take some anyway. I climb into bed while my uncle gets me a ginger ale, and then he leaves so I can fall asleep. As soon as he's gone downstairs, I jump out of bed and check the closet. The bag is still there, the evidence still inside. Relieved, I fall back into bed, suddenly tired. Massively tired.

But of course I don't fall asleep. My mind is racing. I try closing my eyes and taking deep breaths. It doesn't work. I finally give up trying and prepare for a long night. The book I've been reading but haven't touched in over a week seems like a good distraction. Settling into the bed again, I find where I left off.

And that's when my eyes grow heavy, and I finally fall into a much-needed, if fitful, sleep.

THIRTY-FOUR

I'm dreaming. In it, I'm fighting Alan Harder for control of the gun. If I can just get it from him, my parents will be saved. We go back and forth. It's getting fierce. And then, suddenly, there's Charlie standing behind him, eating soft serve from a cone. "Help me!" I yell at her, but instead, she just stands there, telling me, "Let's go do the zip line." I'm about to plead for her help again when I feel the gun yanked out of my hand. I look down, and now I'm holding a dripping snow cone, the sticky liquid trickling out and onto my hands. I hear Charlie say, "Come on, Alden, you know soft serve tastes better than a snow cone." Harder has the gun now and is about to kill my mom and dad. I throw down the snow cone, ready to jump between them and Harder, ready to take the bullets meant for my parents. But Harder is no longer there; Greg Matthes has the gun, and he's pointing it at me, and as everything slows down—Greg pulling the trigger, the gun firing, the bullet coming toward me—I hear myself shouting to Charlie, like the hero in an overly melodramatic movie thriller, "If I couldn't save my parents, at least I can save Amy…"

I wake up to my cell phone ringing. The clock next to my bed says it's a quarter after seven. Who's calling me so early in the morning when there's no school? The name of the caller reads Amy Sloan. I grab it.

"Amy? What is it?"

"Nope, not Amy. Try again."

I've never heard his voice on my phone, but it's not hard to figure out who it is. "Greg? What do you want?"

"I've already told you what I want, Alden. I want you to return what's mine."

I try bluffing. "It's too late. I've already given all of it to the police chief."

"Oh, I hope that's not true. For her sake."

Her sake? "Where's Amy?"

"Funny you should ask." I hear a rustling on the other end of the phone. Then another voice. "I'm so sorry, Alden."

Amy.

"I was so angry, I had to confront him. Make him tell me what he did. Why he did it." She's babbling. "I should never have gone to him." Scared. "I wasn't thinking. I'm so sorry—"

More rustling cuts her off. Then Greg is back. "*I'm so sorry, Alden,*" Greg mimics in a high-pitched voice.

"What do you want?" I say in a trembling voice.

"Haven't you been listening?" Greg taunts. "I want my stuff back."

"Don't hurt her."

"Well, you have a say in that. Bring me my stuff and I won't. Don't, and I will. I'm pretty sure you know how bad."

"I'll bring it. Where do we meet?"

"Miller's Park. How's that for irony? Oh, and Alden, bring all of it. Amy told me about the clothes. And the phone. Bring that, too."

"Okay. Just don't hurt her."

"*Don't hurt her,*" he mimics me now. "Oh, and one more thing. Your notebook. I'm gonna need that, too."

I hear Amy's voice in the background. "I told him everything, Alden. I'm sorry. He made me—" A sudden slap cuts her off.

"I said don't hurt her!"

"That? That was nothing," Greg snarls. "It'll be much worse if you don't get here in twenty minutes."

"I'll need more time than that." With Uncle Bill just down the hall, I lower my voice.

"Sorry. That's all you get. You better hurry."

"I'm coming. I'll bring it right now."

"Good to hear. Oh, and just in case you're planning to call the police or bring your friend…"

All at once, I hear Amy say, "Greg. Please, don't—" She screams.

"Stop it!" I whisper-shout into the phone. "I'll be there! I'm leaving now!" But the line's already dead.

Moving as fast as I ever have in my life, I rush around my room, throwing on the same clothes I wore last night, putting on the same shoes, and getting the bag of evidence. I double-check to make sure everything is inside and hold the phone with the incriminating pictures on it in my hand, considering leaving it here. No, he's sure to check everything in the bag. What if I sent the texts and pictures to my cell phone as a way to hold on to them? But that might take too long. And I have to hurry. He might *kill* her!

I put the phone down on my desk, then pull my notebook out of my desk drawer. I could copy my notes using my printer. Again, too long. I've now got less than twenty minutes. Still, I open my desk drawer and frantically dig around until I find what I'm looking for.

Finally, with phone and notebook in the bag, I creep into the hall, listening for Uncle Bill moving around in his bedroom. I creep down the stairs. There's no sign of him in the living room, kitchen, or back hall. Maybe I've lucked out, and he's gone out for a few minutes. The television is on, showing the morning news, and I stop when I see Alycia Beaumont's face on the screen. A newscaster says, "It has been verified that the body found last night in Powell Lake was that of Alycia Beaumont, who has been missing since last Thursday."

Powell Lake? That's a couple miles from Miller's Park.

"The body had been weighted down," the newscaster continues. "But it was seen by a passerby. Early indications are that, though there was evidence of a head wound, the sixteen-year-old girl may have died of strangulation…"

I want to listen to more, but I've got to go. Just as I reach the door and grab the doorknob, I hear, "Where are you going?"

My uncle stands in the hallway. He's drying his hands with a towel; he must have been in the downstairs bathroom.

My hands are shaking. "I've…g…got to go somewhere," I stutter.

"Are you feeling better?" he asks. "What's in the bag?"

Before I can come up with a response, he notices the expression on my face. "Alden, what's wrong?"

"I'll be back soon."

He steps forward, dropping the towel. "Alden, if something's wrong, you can talk to me about it."

"No, I'm fine. Everything's fine."

"Come on, I can tell something's wrong. Tell me what it is. Let's talk—"

"Why?" I snap at him without thinking. "You only want to talk to me about my father!"

His eyes widen in shock. "What—"

"You say you want to talk about how I'm doing, but all you really want to do is talk about him. But I can't! *I can't!* It's too hard!"

The look on his face makes me wish I could push a button and go back in time to redo these last couple of minutes. What is it about me and the awful things I say to people close to me?

At first, it looks like my uncle doesn't know what to say. But then, in a cracked voice, he says, "I'm sorry. I didn't know you felt that way. But I am your official guardian. I'm responsible for you. So I think you need to tell me where you're going."

Time is rushing by. I have to come up with something. "I'm meeting up with Charlie."

"At this time of the morning?"

I throw out the first thing that comes to my mind. "We're going to buy some junk food, then go back to her house to binge *Westworld*. It'll take all day, so we wanted to start early." My story sounds lame, but it's the best I can come up with.

"You feel like you can eat junk food after last night?"

"I feel better."

"What's in the bag?"

"Just some trash I've been meaning to throw away."

I grab the doorknob again, holding my breath.

"Okay," he says finally. He's going to let me go. I almost let out a sigh of relief. But then he says, "Why don't you give me Charlie's phone number?"

"Why? You have my cell number."

"I've been thinking, I should have some other way to reach you, in case, I don't know, I'm trying to reach you and your phone's not working."

Is he asking because he plans to call Charlie and check on my story? Or does he really just think it's a good idea to have it?

I don't know and I don't care right now. I have to go. "Sure," I say. I give it to him, and he writes it down on an envelope sitting on the side table next to his armchair.

I open the door to leave, but he stops me by saying, "I'm trusting you, Alden."

I look back at him.

"I'm doing the best I can," he says.

"I know you are," I say.

"Call me in a few hours. Just so I know you're okay."

"I will."

"Have fun." The look on his face tells me he's not entirely buying my story, but wants to do the right thing. He wants to be able to trust me.

I go outside, closing the door behind me.

For a split second, I consider going back in and telling him everything. Pass the responsibility on to him and let him take over, so I can curl up and wait to see what happens.

But I can't. I've got less than fifteen minutes. If I'm late, will Greg kill Amy? I feel sure he will. And it'll be my fault. I caused this. I need to take responsibility for it. I need to fix it.

Whether Uncle Bill calls Charlie now to check on my story or waits a few hours for me to check in with him, it doesn't matter. What matters is that I get to Amy.

Before it's too late.

THIRTY-FIVE

It's unwieldy trying to pump bike pedals with the bag tied to my handlebars, but it'll be quicker than walking, and I silently thank Charlie for not asking for it back.

Fortunately, I don't pass that many people. Empty buildings pop up on either side as I slow down near the park's entrance. Breathing hard, I untie the bag, letting the bike fall on its side, before I head in.

I'm five minutes late. Will Greg really have killed her because of five minutes?

The two baseball fields look as barren as the last two times I was here. Abandoned. A place no one comes to anymore, or ever will.

The perfect place for a double murder.

What now? I don't see any sign of Greg or Amy.

"Don't stop!" It's Greg's voice. "Keep coming. To the second field." As I approach the spot where a week ago Alycia had been waiting for Greg, I hear him call out, "Over here. Behind the wall."

Did Greg plan it this way just to be cute? Behind the wall I find Greg and Amy. Greg has one arm around her shoulders, holding her in place. In his other hand, he holds a gun, which he has pressed against her head. His grin is jagged and sharp.

Between us is a hole dug several feet into the ground. Scrunched-up paper and a few pieces of wood lay at the bottom of it. Nearby is a shovel and some other items.

"You took your time getting here," Greg sneers. "It's been more than twenty minutes. You're lucky she's still alive."

"I know. I'm sorry. I did the best I could." To Amy, I ask, "Are you okay?"

She nods, teary-eyed. "This is all my fault, Alden. I should have just waited till this morning to go to the police, like we said. But I was so mad at him for cheating on me, for strangling that poor girl, killing her, I told myself I had to confront him. I should have never—"

"Shut up!" Greg shakes her by the neck.

Amy cries out. She's so scared she's physically trembling. And I'm the one who got her into this. "It's okay," I try to assure her.

"Let's get this over with," Greg says. He points at the hole. "Empty the bag in there." When I don't move right away, he pushes the gun against Amy's head, and she whimpers in pain. "Hurry!" he says.

"I'm hurrying," I say. "Just be careful with that gun. Don't hurt her."

"What's the matter, you got a crush on her? You wish she was your girlfriend? Fat chance. Now get moving. But hand me the notebook first. I want to make sure you're not trying to trick me by throwing in a fake one."

Quickly, I open the bag and hand him the notebook. Then I empty the rest into the hole. Greg's backpack and clothing. The cell phone.

"Very good," he says, finished with the notebook and tossing it into the hole on top of everything else. He peers in and says, "Damn, I liked that backpack. And you dug into our trash to get my clothes? That's creepy."

He catches me staring at the gun and says, "What, you don't believe it's real? It's real."

"Here." He kicks at one of the items on the ground. A can of lighter fluid. "Pick it up." He waves the gun. "Pour it over everything in there." He returns the gun to the side of Amy's head and presses hard. She winces. "Don't think about doing anything funny with that."

Popping off the top of the can with shaking hands, I squeeze it over the hole. "More," he says, and I do it again. The smell of the fluid is overwhelming.

"Drop it and back off," Greg orders. "Don't you try anything."

He lets go of Amy, but still points the gun in her direction as he pulls out a lighter from one of his pockets. I debate trying to jump him as he juggles the gun while crouching down to grab the two rags also laying on the ground, but Amy is too close. Judging from the smell, the rags are already doused in fluid. The first one flares up quickly as he lights it and tosses it into the hole. The second one flares up just as quickly, and he tosses it in as well. Then, grabbing Amy again, he backs up from the rising flames. I stay where I am, staring sadly at the rapidly deteriorating evidence Charlie and I had worked so hard to collect.

Quietly, almost solemnly, we wait until all that's left in the hole are smoldering ashes. There is one more item left on the ground near Greg: a gallon jug of water, which he orders me to use to douse the embers.

None of us say anything for another minute as we watch the smoke spiral up and trail off into the air. Then Greg kicks the shovel. "Now cover up the hole."

Amy looks at him. I pick up the shovel. "What are you going to do with us?" I ask.

Greg's smile is more like a sneer. "Well, that's a good question." He seems to be enjoying himself. "I could do whatever I want, couldn't I? So you start putting the dirt back in that hole, and we'll see what I come up with."

I begin shoveling, realizing he's given me a weapon. He's got the gun firmly in hand, though at least he's not pointing it at Amy now, and I wonder if I can surprise him enough to swing and hit him before he has time to fire it. I keep a close eye on them from the periphery of my vision. Amy still looks scared. When I only have two or three shovelfuls left, she says to Greg, "What are you planning to do with us?"

"I've been thinking about that." I drop another bit of dirt into what's left of the hole as he continues. "I've decided that when he finishes, you can both leave."

This makes me stop and look at him. Amy seems more surprised than I am. "What do you mean, leave?" she says.

"Uh...you should consider yourself...uh...consider yourself lucky." Greg seems confused all of a sudden. Like an actor who's suddenly forgotten his lines and is improvising.

"You're not going to kill him?" Amy says.

"I'm not going to kill...either of you," Greg says. "There's no need." He points at the hole. "The evidence is burned. Gone. With no proof, nobody's going to believe him. Him...or you."

I shovel in the last bit of dirt.

The gun is at his side. He's barely paying any attention to it. His focus is all on Amy.

"Look," Greg is saying. "I told you before—"

All at once, I move, swinging the shovel over and up, the dirt hitting him perfectly in the face. He cries out, bringing one hand to his face, the gun still in his right hand. "Run, Amy!" I shout as I swing again, the spade hitting him just above his right wrist.

"Ow!" he shouts, dropping the gun. I twist around and discover Amy hasn't moved. "Run!" I shout again. "Do you have your cell? Get out of here and call the police!"

She finally starts moving and, holding the shovel firmly across my body, I turn my attention back to Greg. He's holding his damaged hand, the one he throws baseballs with, I note with some perverse satisfaction. He looks at me, his eyes widening into what looks like actual fear. "Get away from me!" he shouts, backing up.

The gun lays in the dirt behind him. I move forward, forcing him to take two steps back. I feint left, and he jumps away to avoid the shovel. I do it again, dancing him back a couple more steps. The shovel is an extension of my hand now, swinging again, missing him on purpose as he ducks. I'm only a couple of steps from the gun, and as he rises up, I swing the shovel once more, letting go of it this time. He grunts as it connects and I leap for the gun.

For a split second, it's like I'm back at the summer fair again, and I'm reaching for the bag with the gun in it, and this time I get it before Alan Harder can. Only when I turn, I'm in Miller's Park, gun in hand, and Greg Matthes is charging toward me. I try to move out of his reach while pointing the gun at him, but he hits me and we both go tumbling, the gun flying out of my hand.

Then we're both up and facing each other. I look for the gun but don't see it. I don't see the shovel, either. And I don't see Amy. Good. At least she's gotten away.

With his good hand, Greg is rubbing his shoulder. "Let's talk about this," he says. The gun glints in the grass, near the other end of the dugout wall. "I was never planning to kill you," he says. "Or Amy. I just wanted to get rid of the evidence so no one would believe you. That's all. Killing Alycia was an accident."

I move to my left, and he moves to block me.

"Look," he says, "all that tough guy stuff I was doing, now and after I cornered you after school yesterday, it was just an act."

I feint to my right, and he copies me.

"I really was going to let you go."

I fake left, then quickly cut right and start running. He tries to react, but I manage to get past him, avoiding his reaching arm, and I dash toward the gun. When I'm almost there, I glance back and gleefully realize he's not going to reach me in time.

Just as my fingers encircle the gun, something slams into the back of my head.

I go tumbling to the ground, thinking, "How did Greg reach me so fast?" Before I can get back up my head explodes again, and, this time, I black out.

THIRTY-SIX

The first thing I notice is how bad my head hurts. Blood trickles down the side of my face from a nasty wound behind my ear. The next thing I notice is how bright the sun is. So bright it hurts. I look away, but it still feels like the light is a knife slipping through the cut on my head to attack the inside of my skull. The pain is so intense it's making me nauseous. I remember now being hit in the head. Twice. By Greg? No, it had to have been a third person. Someone I didn't know was here. Maybe Amy didn't know, either. I'm glad she got away. How much time before help arrives?

Any movement causes the light in my head to slice deeper into my brain. I try to be still, but the ground seems to be doing a slow spin, making me dizzy and disoriented.

Someone is talking. Maybe focusing on them will help reduce the pain. I make out two voices. And now I see two figures. They're not talking so much as arguing. I know I blacked out, but it must not have been for long. Everything's a blur, and trying to cut through it to see the two figures only makes my pain and nausea worse. I close my eyes and try just to listen.

Slowly, the words become clear. "You didn't have to hit him like that." The first voice is male.

"If you'd done what you were supposed to, I wouldn't have had to hit him."

"What if he's dead?"

"I hope he is. That was the plan, wasn't it? What were you doing giving him the shovel?"

A sudden stab of pain in my head almost makes me cry out. I bite my lip to stop from groaning.

"I was improvising. I figured *he* could fill up the hole himself."

"You gave him a *weapon*! You were supposed to just shoot him."

"That was *your* plan." The first voice again. It's Greg. "It's my dad's gun. He'll notice it's been fired. I thought we could try... something else."

"You agreed to it." The second voice is female. But who? Who else could be involved in this?

"I never actually said—"

"By being here, by calling him and setting this up, you agreed to it. You killed Alycia, you can kill him!"

"But Alycia was an accident."

"You hit her with a bag full of books."

"I didn't mean to. This…killing Alden… This is murder."

Razor-edged fingers crawl down my spine.

"We've been through all this. You have to."

"Damn it, I'm not going to do it."

"Don't you curse at me. You know I hate that."

Silence.

Then Greg's voice responds. "I'm sorry, Amy."

He didn't have to say her name for me to realize who the mystery girl is. My gut churns as I finally piece it together, my mind and my heart doing battle because as much as I don't want to believe it, there's no denying I was as wrong about Amy as a person can be.

"You know I don't like it when you curse."

"Yes, I know. I said I was sorry."

Another silence.

Amy didn't run away to get help. She stayed, probably hid on the field side of the dugout wall while I was fighting Greg. And when I got close to the gun, she came out and hit me with the shovel.

This whole thing was a setup. The so-called argument on the way to school that got me to talk to her, Greg treating her badly at his locker. Her telling me how Greg had changed. Her shock when I told her Greg was a murderer. Amy acting on the phone like Greg was hurting her. All of it fake, an act. I'd been trying to save her, but Amy had already known what her boyfriend had done and has been helping him cover it up.

Some investigator I am.

I try not to move. I just listen.

Amy's voice comes back. "Do you really think even with the evidence destroyed, he won't say anything?"

"No one would believe him," Greg argues. "A lot of people think he got weird after what happened to his parents."

"It only takes a few."

"If we threatened him—"

"Threatened him. Really? You mean like you tried to do?"

"Threaten to tell the people he's been spying on. Threaten to tell Rick what Alden wrote about him. If it's true, Rick won't want people to know. He'll beat the shit out of Alden."

"Language!"

"All right. Beat the *crap* out of him. But you and I are the ones who know what he wrote. We could threaten to tell all of them."

Another part of the lie. Rick Kellerman *didn't* notice me following him. Amy only knew because Greg had read it in my notebook and told her about it. She'd been toying with me.

"Rick's a big macho wrestler, but he likes fashion," Amy says. "Big deal. Besides, you don't have the notebook anymore, you burned it. You had to. Alden could just deny he'd had a notebook."

Greg mumbles something I can't make out, but it sounds like he's still not down with the whole Kill Alden plan. *Come on, Greg. Come on. Stand up to her. I don't want to die. Please.* Then comes another pause. Longer this time. I consider opening my eyes to see what's happening.

Finally, Amy starts talking again. "I wouldn't have gone on to church camp if I didn't think you could handle this. You should have gotten rid of that backpack right away, or at least as soon as you read the notebook."

"I didn't think I had time after we dumped Alycia's body, so I hid it in the best place I could. I figured I'd get rid of it later. How the hell should I have known this dweeb was stalking me, for Christ's sake?"

"Do *not* use the Lord's name in vain!" She sounds like she's freaking out. "How many times do I have to tell you—?"

"Oh, come on, Amy!"

"You know how I *hate* that!"

Greg says nothing.

"You know what you have to do," she says.

"I think he's dead already," Greg grumbles.

"He's not. I can see him breathing. Kill him and we'll dump his body in Powell Lake like we did Alycia's. No one will ever find them."

Apparently, neither of them saw the news this morning.

I hear Greg take a shaky breath. "Alycia's death was an accident."

"You keep saying that."

"I didn't mean to kill her."

"Try telling the police that when they arrest you."

"This is different. I can't do it. I'm sorry."

"You're sorry?" Amy snaps, her voice rising as she continues. "You should have been sorry about cheating on me with that girl. Because none of this would have happened if you hadn't done that!"

"I told you I was sorry. I wanted to stop. But she had those pictures…"

"I wanted to be your first," Amy says, her voice suddenly quiet. "And you mine. When the time was right. When we knew for sure we were the right one for each other."

"I made a mistake," Greg says.

The steel returns to her voice. "And now it's time to remedy it."

"I…can't…"

Amy loses it. "Do I have to do *everything* for you?" She takes several deep breaths, maybe to get herself under control. "Do I have to remind you where you would be if not for me? In jail, that's where. Your solution after you hit her was to run away. What would you have done if she hadn't called me before she called you?"

My God. How deep did Amy's involvement go?

"I told you, I didn't know she'd done that," Greg murmurs.

My investigative mind kicks into overdrive: There had been no other phone number on the burner. Just Greg's. She must have called Amy on her regular phone.

She left a trail.

"Of course you didn't. She acted all innocent, claimed she hadn't know about us, when all along she just wanted me to see you two together. Prove what she told me on the phone—that you were tired of waiting for me and found someone better."

The anger I hear in Amy's voice is something I never thought I'd hear from her. "Girls like her don't understand why waiting is important. But I thought you understood, Greg."

"It wasn't like that—"

Amy talks right through him. "Then you make it worse by killing her. If I hadn't shown up when I did, you would have eventually wimped out and told the police. You needed me to show you a way out of this. I did that."

Greg didn't lose Amy's necklace. *She* lost it. She got here after Greg killed Alycia, and the clasp broke, and the necklace fell off while she was helping him move Alycia Beaumont's body. By the time she realized it was gone, she didn't know when she had lost it, or where, and didn't have time to look since she was already late getting to church camp. Maybe she told Greg to look, but if he did, it wasn't until after Charlie and I had searched the park and found it. Meanwhile, Amy spent the weekend at camp acting like nothing had happened. The cut on her head really was from walking into a tree branch while she was there, I guess.

"All you had to do was get rid of the evidence," Amy is saying. "But you couldn't even do that right. I can't believe you didn't delete everything off that phone! How could you be so stupid? Or maybe you really wanted to keep those pictures. Do you know how awful it was for me, seeing them for the first time when Alden showed them to me?"

All the pieces fall together in my mind; I know what really happened, and I see how wrong I was, how easily Amy played me.

Yet while listening to Milton High School's perfect couple fall apart like this, I can't help but feel like there's something I'm missing. Something I can't put my finger on. Maybe I'm only imagining it. The way my head is spinning, it's amazing I'm able to think at all.

"Take the gun, Greg."

"Amy, I…I can't…"

Is it something I heard? It feels like something I should know. Something I *would* know if my head didn't hurt so much.

"You started this. You finish it."

I have to do something. Move, if I can, though I'm not even sure I can get up. I open my eyes and, through the blur, see Greg, now with the gun in his hand, turning slowly toward me.

It keeps tugging at me. Something I heard on the news report this morning.

"I don't want to kill anybody, Amy," Greg says, sounding like a six-year-old who doesn't want to drink his milk.

Something Amy said while she was pretending to be scared when Greg was holding the gun on her.

Amy snaps back at him. "You should have thought of that before you killed that girl!"

That's it!

Greg brings the gun up.

"Did you strangle her, Greg?" I blurt out.

Greg stops, holding the gun straight out. They both stare at me with their mouths open in surprise.

"He's awake," Amy says. "He's been faking it, listening to us all this time. Shoot him!"

Just the act of talking makes my head pound, but I push through it. "Did you strangle Alycia Beaumont, Greg?"

"What? No!"

I manage to lift my arm enough to point at Amy. "*She* said you did."

"She…what?"

"Will you just kill him already?" Amy snarls.

"She said it right after I got here," I spit out through gritted teeth. "*Did* you strangle her, Greg?"

"No. I just hit her with my backpack."

"Stop listening to him! Pull the trigger!" Amy's voice has taken on an additional edge.

"But she *was* strangled," I tell Greg, struggling to my knees. "It was on the news this morning. Her body was found in Powell Lake last night."

Amy's head snaps toward me in surprise. Greg says, "They found her?"

"He's lying," Amy barks.

I plow forward, fighting nausea, my attention focused on Greg as best I can. "Yes, she'd had a head wound. But the news reported there were marks on her neck that looked like…signs of strangulation. The police think it's possible that's what killed her. Not the head wound."

Greg's hand holding the gun drops to his side. "But I didn't strangle her," he says.

"They said it's 'possible,'" Amy retorts. "But they don't know. There could be other reasons for marks on her neck. Or maybe you grabbed her neck first, then hit her with the backpack."

"I thought you said I was lying," I tell Amy. Her head snaps back at me, anger blazing in her eyes.

"I didn't grab her neck. I'm sure of it," Greg says. "We were arguing, getting louder, and next thing I knew I was swinging my books over my head at her, and she hit the wall. I dropped the backpack, and she fell."

"He's just trying to confuse you—"

"I didn't strangle her," Greg says, more emphatic now.

"How did she know, Greg?" I say.

For the first time since I came to, Amy looks flustered. "I…saw it on the news this morning. Just like you did."

"No, that's not true," I say. "You were talking about dumping me in Powell Lake, just like you did with Alycia. You said no one would ever find us. You didn't know her body had already been found."

Another first: Amy struggling for a comeback.

"How did you know Alycia was strangled?" I ask.

"Yes, Amy," Greg says, turning toward her. "How did you know?"

Amy says nothing, her back ramrod straight.

"Because she's the one who strangled her," I say to Greg. "She got here soon after you ran off. Because, like she said, Alycia didn't just call you, Greg. She called her. Timed their meeting so Amy would find you together. Alycia thought she could manipulate you. But she hadn't counted on you getting violent."

The world spins a bit, and I wince, but continue. "What Amy finds instead is Alycia on the ground, bleeding. Maybe awake but hurt. Maybe unconscious, but definitely still breathing. It's easy to figure out what happened; did you leave your backpack, which, of course, she recognized? Is that what caused you to come back?"

"Yes," Greg says, after several seconds. "But I also thought I might have been wrong about her being dead. I thought if she wasn't, I could help her. Call an ambulance. Or maybe it wasn't even as bad as I thought. But when I got back…" He looks at Amy.

"Amy was there," I say. "Telling you she found Alycia like this. Telling you *you* killed her. But don't worry, she said. She loved you so much, she'd help you get rid of the body. Because she would do anything for you. Is that what she told you, Greg? And you believed her? She was really doing it for herself. Because she's the one who killed her. She took advantage of the situation and strangled Alycia until she really was dead."

It's taken just about all the energy I have left to get all that out, and I roll onto my side. By the look on Amy's face, if I didn't get all of it right, I got most of it. I don't know what's going to happen next, but if it's bad, I'm not sure I have the strength to stop it.

Greg has turned back to Amy, the gun still down by his side. "Why did you do it?" he asks her, his voice dull and distant.

"Greg…"

"*Why did you do it, Amy?*"

To her credit, Amy doesn't flinch. At first it even looks like she might try to keep up the act and deny everything.

But then her expression changes, her eyes turning dark as her usually sweet face hardens into something cold. "You and I had everything," she hisses, "and you threw it away because you couldn't wait? Sex was more important to you than what we had? When she called, she was especially sure to tell me about the pictures. Because she felt so awful about it, she said, and thought I should know. She didn't feel awful. She did it to dig at me, to gloat. That's the kind of girl you'd gotten yourself involved with."

When Greg doesn't respond, her tone and expression changes again, to something between pleading and trying to sound reasonable. "I did it for you, Greg. For both of us. So that no one would ever have to know. Everyone looks up to us. We have to set an example."

"I might have been able to save her."

"Oh, please, stop telling yourself that. You just wanted to get your backpack, maybe see if she had the phone on her, which fortunately she did, or we'd have really been in trouble. I saw your face; you were relieved she was dead."

"You're wrong. I was sorry I hit her. I would've—"

"So sorry you went along with my plan to cover it up?"

Greg starts to object. But then he stops and turns away from her. Amy hesitates, then moves toward him, placing her hand tentatively on his back. "Greg, we can still get out of this." She points at me. "If he's dead, nobody will know."

I find the energy to get back to my knees. "You haven't killed anybody yet, Greg." My pounding heart competes with the throbbing in my head. "You didn't mean to kill Alycia, and you didn't." I try pointing at Amy, but this time it feels like I'm trying to control a wet noodle. "*She* killed her."

"You think that's going to make a difference to the police?" Amy counters. "Kill him. We'll figure out some other way to get rid of his body. We'll find someplace to bury him, like we just did with the evidence. Then we'll never talk about it again. We'll go back to normal, and no one will ever know."

"Normal," Greg mutters. Amy moves in behind him, wrapping both arms around his waist, her hands hanging tantalizingly close to the front of his jeans, below his belt buckle. "If you really want to, I'd even be willing to…you know."

"Jesus!" Greg explodes, pushing her away and turning. "Don't do that. What makes you think we can ever be normal again? I'm not going to shoot him, Amy. I'm not." He tosses the gun on the ground.

Bad move. Amy jumps and picks it up. Then she points it at me. "If you're not going to do it," she barks, "then I will!"

"Amy…"

"You're not going to stop me, Greg."

My knees give out and I flop onto the ground, unable to even try to crawl away. I'm not as scared about the prospect of dying as I thought I'd be. It just means I'm going to get to see my parents very soon.

I just wish I could have said goodbye to Charlie. To Uncle Bill.

"Amy…"

"I'm doing this for both of us."

I close my eyes.

"Amy, I didn't…"

I hear a click and my insides shrivel, followed a second later by another click, then more, one right after the other.

Amy's shouting, almost hysterical now. "You didn't *load* it? You didn't put the *bullets* in the *gun*?"

"I couldn't. I'm sorry. I told you. I'm not a killer."

"You idiot. You—"

I open my eyes, expecting to see Amy rushing toward me, ready to strangle me. But what I see is Amy collapsing on the ground, crying as if it's the end of her world. Which, in a way, I guess it is.

I see Greg standing over her; he's not trying to comfort her. He's just staring, his face a combination of disgust and terrible pain.

And then, all at once, Miller's Park is filled with the sounds of police sirens, police lights flashing, the voice of Chief Walker shouting, "Over here, over here!"

I try to stand, getting almost all the way up before I start to fall again, my dizzying head about to explode.

And somehow, miraculously, Charlie is there to catch me, her strong arms cradling me gently to the ground. "I'm here, Alden," she murmurs into my ear. "I'm here."

A police officer takes the never-loaded gun out of Amy's hand and another officer helps her to her feet as she continues to cry inconsolably. It sounds like she will never stop. Another officer has her hands on Greg's arms, leading him away as Greg hangs his head.

"Just hang in there," I hear Charlie say. Then she says, "What's with the shovel?"

"The evidence," I manage, my mouth feeling heavy and mushy. "They made me throw it in a hole and burn it, then bury the embers."

"Aw, man. All that work…"

"It's okay," I mumble, fumbling in my pants pocket.

"What? What is it?"

I manage to pull out the cell phone and hand it to Charlie. "There are pictures on here."

"Pictures?" she asks.

"You'll see. More evidence."

"You didn't burn it?"

"I switched it with the phone you bought."

"The burner phone?"

"Yeah. I know I was supposed to get rid of it after I called the police, but I never did. Greg checked to make sure I hadn't switched notebooks, but he never thought to check the phone I threw."

I can sense Charlie smiling. "That's my Alden," she says. "Always thinking."

She gives me a soft kiss on the cheek.

From somewhere in the distance, Chief Walker shouts, "Paramedics! Over here!"

Followed by Uncle Bill crying, "Alden, Alden!"

A good investigator knows when to call it a day.

The paramedics carry me into an ambulance. But for the few brief seconds before they get here, there is no other place I'd rather be than in Charlie's arms.

THIRTY-SEVEN

It's three days before I'm able to talk to Charlie again. It turns out not only do I have a level two concussion, I have a fractured skull. It's not as bad as it sounds—my skull will heal naturally over the next six to eight weeks. Still, the hospital keeps me in intensive care for the first day and a half, making me go through two CAT scans to check for brain swelling. Fortunately, they don't find any. Various medical people come in to poke and prod me, and give me verbal exercises I should, under normal circumstances, be able to do. I admit, for the first day, I struggle to do them. But by halfway through the second day I'm much better at it, and I'm moved to my own room, where the lights are kept dim. I'm ordered to rest and am only allowed out of bed to go to the bathroom, with help. Doctors come to see me regularly.

Uncle Bill has been with me the entire time, sleeping the few chances he gets either on the single chair in the ICU or on the narrow, hard, couch-like piece of furniture in my room. I doze often, and every time I wake up, he's there.

At one point, when he thinks I'm sleeping, I say to him, "I'm sorry."

My uncle puts down the magazine he's been reading and leans toward me. "You have no reason to be sorry."

"I should have told you where I was really going."

"It's okay. You were trying to help someone you thought was in trouble."

"And for saying what I said about you always wanting to talk about my father. It was…cruel."

"You were upset. It's okay."

"It's not. I'm sorry the way I've treated you. You've been trying your best and most of the time I've been—"

He cuts me off. "Alden. Listen. I know it hasn't been easy for you," he says. "There are things I wish I had done differently. There's a lot I'm still learning about being a parent."

"I've got a lot to learn, too," I say. "Maybe we can help each other."

"Yeah." Uncle Bill nods his head. "That would be nice."

"And I'd like you to tell me more about my father," I say. "When he was my age."

"Sure. And maybe, if it's okay with you, Alden, I'd like to talk with you about what happened at the fair that day. The police told me, of course, but I never heard it from you. I'd like to know what my brother's last day was like, you know, before it happened. Your mother's, too."

"Yes," I say. "Give me a little time but...yeah. I can do that."

"Thank you."

"There is one thing I've been wanting to ask you about. Dad wanted to tell me some good news that day," I add. "They were both really happy about it."

"What was it?"

"I don't know. I was hoping maybe you did. He never got the chance to tell me because that's when the guy started firing. I'll never know what it was."

"We can talk about that later, too, if you'd like."

"Yeah. Okay." But now I'm not sure it matters anymore whether I know or not.

The next day, my third day in the hospital, Chief Walker comes by to tell me that any questions he has can wait until after I'm discharged and home. Especially since both Greg and Amy have confessed. "Someday, though," he says, "you and I are going to have a talk about what you were doing. And why you shouldn't have done it."

"Yes, sir." I figured this talk would be coming.

"You were lucky," he says. "Remember that. But you're also smart. You never know, with the proper training, when you're *older*, of course—like after you've finished high school and college—maybe you could become a very good investigator." With that, he gives me a smile. "Just not yet, okay?"

Still smiling, he leaves the room.

A little later Charlie shows up. I'm so happy to see her. Uncle Bill is in the room, and he excuses himself, saying he'll get himself some coffee and maybe a bite to eat. He should probably go home and sleep, but I know I won't be able to convince him to do that.

As Charlie sits in the chair he just vacated, my uncle looks back at me from the door and gives me a smile and a wink.

"How are you feeling?" Charlie asks.

"Better," I say. "Your father was here earlier."

"Yeah, I know," she answers, smiling. "You're not going to have to testify, it looks like. Greg couldn't wait to confess. Amy lasted a day before she caved."

"It's hard to get my head around the thought of Amy Sloan killing someone."

"I know. I liked her. I keep thinking about their parents. Their families. How hard it must be on them."

I think back to Greg's little sister; she clearly looked up to him. How was she handling it?

It had to be harder for Alycia Beaumont's family, though. Did she have a sister or brother? Had her parents spent those days waiting for news on their daughter hoping and praying she would be okay? What were they feeling now, with those hopes dashed and their prayers unanswered?

So many lives altered, changed forever. It's difficult to think about.

"What's that?" I ask Charlie. She has a bag in her hand.

"I bought the entire series of *Criminal Minds* on DVD. We've been talking about bingeing it."

"We can watch it on Netflix."

"I figured you should own it. It'll be good training for you when you get back to being an investigator."

"It's twelve seasons or more. New episodes are still on every week."

"So it'll take a while."

"I don't think I'm going to be able to watch much TV until my head is better."

She shrugs and puts the bag on the table next to my bed. "Whenever you're ready."

I look at her. "Thank you."

"I wondered when you were going to say that." Charlie smiles. "You're welcome, you big goof."

"You're bigger than I am," I respond.

"Bigger and stronger. But not goofier."

I smile back at her.

We sit in silence for a few seconds. "Do you know when they're letting you out of here?" Charlie asks.

"Probably tomorrow. I'm still supposed to rest, though. Come back to see the doctors. I'm going to be out of school for two weeks. Then my classes will be limited after that."

"By the time you're back to a normal schedule, the school year will be over."

"I may need to take a couple of refresher classes early in the summer, then take finals."

"Ah, you'll do fine. You've got great grades. You could probably pass finals right now, even with a concussion."

"Thanks, but I think I'll be happy with taking things one day at a time for now."

"Good plan." She leans in. "Everybody's talking about you at school, you know."

"Good things?" I ask.

"You're super detective Alden Ross."

"More like Alden Ross, Cry-Wolf Boy."

"I don't think you have to worry about those first two calls. They're ancient history, and understandable. My father knows when to keep certain things to himself."

"Still, I think I should apologize to Gavin."

"Yeah, maybe." Again, Charlie leans in. "I don't know if I should be telling you this, but I heard how they got Alycia Beaumont's body to Powell Lake. Neither Alycia or Greg have their own cars, but with Amy's parents out of town, she went home and got her mother's car.

This was after they threw Alycia's body over the right-field fence into some bushes. Greg was hiding with the body outside of the field when the police showed up after you called them. Doesn't say much for our police force, does it?"

"They figured it was a false alarm," I offer.

"Yeah, well, my father made sure they knew he wasn't happy about it. Anyway, when Amy was back with the car and something to wrap the body in and to weight it down, they drove to Powell Lake and dropped poor Alycia in the water. They're lucky nobody saw them, though it's pretty empty out there. They had one of Greg's parents' cars parked close by to do the same thing with you. Cold, huh?"

"Yeah," I say. "Except Greg didn't want to kill me. By not loading the gun, he saved my life."

"Hadn't thought of that," Charlie says.

"I never heard how you got there with the police when you did," I ask.

"Your uncle called me to check that you were with me," she says.

"I guess I'm glad he didn't trust me."

"When he said you had a big bag with you, I knew it was the evidence," Charlie continues. "I didn't know why you still had it, so I asked him more questions. When he said Amy had come by the day before, I got suspicious. That argument she and Greg had on the way to school for all to see, especially you, seemed fishy to me. Staged."

"They fooled me," I mutter. "Especially Amy. Played me for a sucker."

"Ah, don't be too hard on yourself. You just have a softer heart than I do. Anyway, I told my dad everything. It was my idea to check Miller's Park. Criminals returning to the scene of the crime and all that."

"I'm glad you did," I tell her. "Told your dad, I mean."

My head is starting to hurt again. It should be time for me to rest. I want to close my eyes, but I don't want Charlie to leave.

She suddenly has a serious look on her face. "I'm sorry," she says.

"For what?"

"For not being there for you. For abandoning you when you needed me the most. When you realized it was the girl from Carlson who'd been killed, you should have felt like you could call me. That was my fault for making you feel that way."

"But I understand why," I say. "I think I might have been a little out of control by then. And then I said some really awful stuff to you."

"Still," Charlie says. "Water under the bridge. We're partners, aren't we?"

"Sure," I say without hesitation. "Not that we'll be doing any investigating in the future. I messed up a lot. I think my investigating days are over."

"Oh, I don't know about that." Charlie grins. "You're the one who figured out it was Amy who killed Alycia Beaumont, not Greg."

Alycia Beaumont. It was strange how we didn't know each other and never would, and yet our lives had become so intertwined. What if I hadn't panicked and run the day Alycia died? I could have seen she was still alive. Maybe I could have saved her.

Truth is, I'll never know. Just like I'll never know if I would have saved my parents had I gone to Chief Walker right away, or to any of the police at the fair, and told them about the suspicious man I bumped into, instead of blowing it off and getting in line for a snow cone.

Would it have made any difference? Maybe. Maybe not. We make decisions every day, and often we don't know the full consequences of those decisions until later. Maybe the key is to keep trying to do the best we can. If we can teach ourselves to do that, maybe it'll make it easier to live with our choices. And their consequences.

"What are you so lost in thought about?" Charlie asks.

I'd like to talk to my best friend about this—but at another time, when my head feels less scrambled.

Right on schedule, the nurse comes in with my next dose of pain medicine.

When the nurse leaves, I tell Charlie, "I should probably close my eyes now. Maybe nap a little."

"I'll go." Charlie starts to get up.

"No," I tell her. "Please stay. Do you mind?"

She looks at me. "Of course not."

"I don't think I'll be asleep long."

"Take all the time you need. I'll be here."

As I settle in, Charlie leans over and gives me a soft kiss, first on the cheek, then on the corner of my mouth. Then she takes hold of my hand.

I close my eyes.

A good investigator knows when it's time to rest.

Knowing that Charlie will still be here when I wake up helps me drift into what feels like the deepest, most restful sleep I've had in a long time.

ACKNOWLEDGMENTS

Publishing a novel is always a team effort, and I had a great team working with me at Sourcebooks Fire. A big thank-you to my editor, Annie Berger, for your guidance and insight. Thank you also to Sarah Kasman, Cassie Gutman, Nicole Hower (who designed the awesome cover), Lynne Hartzer, and Alex Yeadon. You guys are the best (and my sincere apologies to anyone I might have missed). In addition, thank you to my fellow authors of the KidLit Authors Club. Your support and friendship always means so much. As always, a heartfelt thank-you to my wonderful agent, Wendy Schmalz, to whom this book is dedicated. And finally, and most of all, to my wife, Janet, and my son, Will, whose love and support makes this all possible.

ABOUT THE AUTHOR

Jeffry W. Johnston is the author of the Edgar Award–nominated *Fragments* and the In the Margins Book Award winner *The Truth*. Both were YALSA Quick Pick for Reluctant Young Adult Readers selections. He also writes freelance articles on numerous subjects, including film and television. He writes music, plays guitar in a band, and loves movies, reading, baseball (he has always been and always will be a Phillies fan), and bingeing entire television series. He lives in the Philadelphia area with his wife and, when he's home from college, their son.

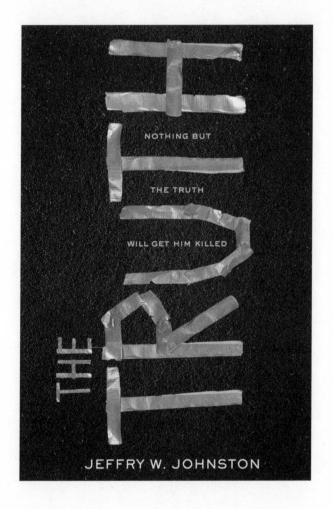

NOTHING BUT THE TRUTH WILL GET HIM KILLED.

"A tough, fast, twisty little brawler of a book."

—*Booklist*

FIREreads

—— @ #getbooklit ——

Your hub for the hottest young adult books!

Visit us online and sign up for our
newsletter at FIREreads.com

@sourcebooksfire

sourcebooksfire

firereads.tumblr.com